THE GATHERING STORM

A novel

THE GATHERING STORM

A novel

Hamza Sokko

MKUKI NA NYOTA
DAR—ES—SALAAM

PUBLISHED BY
Mkuki na Nyota Publishers Ltd
Nyerere Road, Quality Plaza Building
P. O. Box 4246
Dar es Salaam, Tanzania
www.mkukinanyota.com
publish@mkukinanyota.com

First Published by Tanzania Publishing House, 1977
Revised Edition, 2012

ISBN 978 9987 08 202 5

ONE

There is an earth road running straight north of Bulembe. It runs thus for about twenty miles and then it begins to wind its way down the high Anyalungu plateau before it turns east to join Morogoro and ultimately Dar es Salaam.

As you go along this road, you will find an old building just outside Bulembe, it is on the right. Up to this day many people know it by the name of *Boma*, or in those days, the office of the District Commissioner. It stands on a raised brick quadrangle. The place has not undergone much physical change: the several pillars that skirt a narrow verandah running round the building; the old, tall eucalyptus trees that continue to stand, three on each side of it; the long wooden forms that lie on the verandah; the creeping grass on the quadrangle - everything.

The place is physically the same as in the past, but there is a very much different atmosphere about it. In those days not many people, besides the clerks dressed in white and the keen-to-attack D.C.'s messengers, approached. In the mornings it looked an active, immediate enemy. With the messengers looking at you, in their dark blue sweaters and red tarbooshes with tufts of thread flopping over their rims, there was a possibility to see their point of attack and know how escape might have been attempted. But non-office hours were even worse. It was a lonesome place. The building, with its roof raised at the front and slanting to the back, looked like a sleeping lion. It would be deserted during those hours, and of yet there was always a visible alertness registered in the eyes of those who know what the building was.

The tall eucalyptus trees with their branches swaying to and fro, their leaves letting through the pressure of the wind, appeared to sing a sad, endless tale which belonged to that place since its erection early in the past German era. The trees had grown beside the building and had always been there to witness all that had taken place. And each day they recorded in their growing selves all that happened before them.

The tall trees would go on mourning in the same manner and cursing the sleeping lion of a building. Its glass windows shone reflecting everything in its vicinity. To pass near the building and get one's image reflected gave one a fatalistic feeling; for the glass windows looked like cameras ready to snap and put one before their lord to answer the hundred and one accusations one always ran into, consciously or not. The red and white flag of the Queen used to wave without much energy on a flag pole that stood near the edge of the quadrangle. It had no peace, for the steady current sent to it from the swaying and mourning eucalyptus trees disturbed it. The red corrugated-iron sheets suppressed from eruption dark things which persistently fought to come out, with an opposing pressure so vast that it could wreck the building and bury the lifelessly waving flag under its debris.

As long as the Bulembe people could remember, the high plateau had remained uninhabited for ages. The Akolongo people who inhabited the plains below the plateau believed that high plateau was the home of the gods. They called it the land of the Anyalungu. When a person died, the Akolongo believed that he went to serve the Anyalungu on the plateau. He would stay there as a slave of the Anyalungu until they allowed him to return. But fearing that he would tell those on earth all about them, the Anyalungu brought the person back in the form of a newborn baby. Thus when a baby was born, the Akolongo tried their best to trace which of its features resembled those of a dead grandfather. And when they produced more babies than the number of dead grandfathers, they took it that in the land of the Anyalungu the few grandfathers had married and got sons and daughters who then increased the number of babies being born.

When a new baby was born, the Akolongo women kept asking it, "How are the Anyalungu? How do they look?" and so on. But the babies would not say a single thing, and the people took this to be the dumbness given by the Anyalungu.

It is still remembered, too, that there was once a man among the Akolongo called Njunju. This man was punished, by the Akolongo chief for a reason nobody knows up to this day. He was to go to the country of the Anyalungu alive, together with his family. Njunju was given a big escort which sent him almost to the edge of the flat land.

Njunju lived on the plateau for a week or so and he did not see any god. The despair which had gripped him and his family shook off slowly, day after day, and it eventually vanished. He tilled the land and built a durable home and after a year or so he was already established. Many years passed and the population on the plateau increased. On finding that he was prosperous in the land that was thought to belong to the Anyalungu whom he could not see, Njunju, then chief of the new tribe decided to call his tribe the Anyalungu. Thus these Anyalungu went on living there, tilling the fertile plains and ridges. And up to now the indigenous people of Bulembe claim to have descended from Njunju.

Before the invasion of Njunju the land had always been peaceful. Bounded by the steep edges that marked the plateau, and having valleys and gorges isolated from human disturbance, the land had been quietly enjoying the melodies sung by birds and by the currents in its many rivers and streams. In its quiet sleep the land had maintained a law of which it was very much proud. Trees grew together with other types of vegetation. Lions helped themselves to the zebras and other animals.

Vultures and other birds of prey also never missed their chance and lived on the many species of birds and animals. In the fresh waters of the rivers, fish were plentiful. Each living thing helped itself to another for its existence. But a cat never ate a cat nor did a lion eat another lion. No, this didn't happen and this the land didn't dream about.

But the harmony was to be wrecked. There were to come into the silently sleeping land beings who went on two legs. They wouldn't, like the forest trees, let one tree grow and flourish beside another. No, they wouldn't. And unlike the cats, they wouldn't exist at the expense of a mouse and let a fellow cat live without depending upon it. They would exist at the expense of a rat, snake, fish and even a fellow human. Probably in its long sleep of peace the land did not foresee this or otherwise it would have turned into tears the fresh waters that flowed smoothly, singing the endless, sweet lullaby.

The invaders would like to live without the motion of a single limb in an attempt to look for means of existence. Instead they would push one of their species to do it for them, day after day without end.

During the times of the first generations of the early Anyalungu, such a life was led by rare individuals. The Anyalungu called these *chotos*, people who did not know how to handle the hoe. They depended upon others without good reasons. But later on, when a white race invaded the land and plundered the Anyalungu, such habit was not looked upon as a weakness. So many people indulged in it shamelessly. It was not possible any more to pick out who was a *choto* and who was not. Thus the appellation became almost meaningless. What the Anyalungu formerly called a *choto* was then a superior person. It was a time when one would sit at the market in Bulembe beside one's produce, waiting the whole day long, and keep looking very appealingly at the faces of those formerly called *chotos*. These, looked upon as masters, would take pity and slip something into the hand of the poor fellow in tatters and take away all that he had with him in the basket.

Bulembe was a small town. There were no proper streets. Mud houses were just crowded behind lines of shops that marked the edges of a quadrangle. The quadrangle was the market place. It consisted of two tiny buildings surrounded by many canopy-forming mango and almond trees. Very early in the mornings this square would begin to .get filled. Men, together with their women dressed in black calico sheets, or *kaniki* tucked above the breasts, filled the whole market.

The women in black would sit forming black clusters under the mango trees. There was little to talk about and even less to be done. They listened, watched and a few hoped. They sat gazing at their surroundings. For most of the time, they kept their eyes fixed upon the shop buildings whose aluminium roofs dazzled them.

Besides the little noise that came up from the market, the town had its characteristic Indian music which blared from some source that those sitting under the mango trees could not imagine. Whether the Indians were making parties in their houses, or whether it was just a group of Indian girls singing, they would not know. Asian women with their children would be seen bending over the balconies of the few storeyed buildings, dressed in their beautiful saris, and chewing, chewing all the time. In the stillness of the air that hung over the market square, voices penetrated without much interference. One from the balcony of one house would talk to another on the opposite balcony and those in the market shade down below listened attentively to the talk as if they understood what was being said. They knew that they were not concerned and that they did not understand, but they still listened without thinking about it.

It might appear that the Anyalungu women had always been unjustifiably looked upon as foolish, and had been laughed at, for believing in some kind of superb ancestry of the Asian town-dwellers who fascinated them so. But for the Anyalungu, it was nevertheless unimaginable that one would acquire all the status that Asians mysteriously acquired, for a price they didn't see. Even the messengers, who were harsh and haughty to the people, trembled before a mere child occupying one of those wondrous storeyed houses. The pitifulness of the whole situation was symbolized by the foolish smiles and even the feeling of pride and gratefulness of those in black calico to have those idols near them. The worst thing was for a people to be born in the midst of a social situation and never come to know when, how and why it all began to develop.

TWO

The sun shone very brightly one afternoon, sending its hot rays scorching the red soil of Bulembe. The few tinned roofs dazzled the eyes of the small number of persons to be seen in the town. The market place, as usual, was filled with people selling provisions. Noises came up occasionally. Messengers traversed the whole length of the town, time after time, without seeming to get tired. The hot sun kept those walking in its rays oozing sweat that formed tiny rivulets as it flowed down.

The attention of the small town was arrested for a while by the rumble of a lorry that drove down the main road from Dar es Salaam. All eyes were turned to it. Transactions inside the shops were disrupted. People came out and stood on the door steps and verandahs as though ejected by some force.

The open-body passenger lorry pulled up outside the storeyed building south of the market, before a white signboard printed with huge black capitals: B. J. KHANJI & SONS TRANSPORT COMPANY LTD. One man who had been squeezed in a corner since early morning stood up painfully and stretched his limbs. He peeped outside through the slits of the wooden body for a brief while and took his basket to go out. He stood outside the lorry gazing in all directions for a long time. Then, with the hot sun pouring on him, he moved spontaneously to the shade of an almond tree at the edge of the market square. He leaned against the trees, still gazing about.

That was Bulembe. Exactly as it had been some eight years back. He remembered very well the day when he left this place. It was as sunny as the day he saw Bulembe again. Gradually his eyes recorded some changes. Yes. He saw the glimmering roofs of the storeyed buildings. But no, nothing remarkable.

The man gazed at the clusters of women in black who sat some few paces off, the loose red dust everywhere, the messengers of the D.C. who passed him. It was much the same. There was a blank gaze on his face. He looked hard at the clusters. As if in a dream he thought that he could recognize a face. Clasping his basket to his side, he walked with firm steps towards her, with his eyes never leaving his target.

Are you well, mothers?" he greeted them. The women raised their eyes to him hesitatingly. Nobody responded and the greeting got lost in the stillness of the air. One of the women, on seeing that the man kept looking fixedly at her, rose, feeling herself somewhat familiar with his face.

"Nganda," the man called her by name. "Have you forgotten me?" The woman came nearer and with a bend of her knees took the hand the man held out to her.

"You are Shemeji Kamuyuga."

The man smiled broadly with delight. "Are you well, Nganda?"

"We are, somehow," she said with a smile, crouching again on the ground.

"I have just arrived with Khanji." He pointed at the vehicle that was then deserted and lying still as if it had been there all the time. "How are my wife and children?"

"They are well, too. Yesterday your wife, Mugindi, came to sell her bananas. But today she did not come."

"How is my brother Lubele?"

Nganda turned her eyes round searchingly and they rested upon a man in a brown *kanzu*. "He is there. He has finished selling the bananas he carried."

Before Nganda had ceased speaking, Kamuyuga was caught by the arm in a bony grip and he was made to swing round.

"Show your tax chits," the familiar messengers mumbled at him. The soldiers of the D.C. panted heavily. Sweat streamed down their cheeks.

A train of victims trailed behind them. Kamuyuga fumbled in his pockets, fishing out a small bundle of papers. He held it out to one of them. The other snatched the chits and turned them over and over in his hands without looking. He replaced them in the hands of Kamuyuga and, pushing his victims before him, they walked away.

Kamuyuga, who till then had not shown any sign of sweating, lifted his palm and with its back wiped off the tiny drops that had all of a sudden accumulated over his forehead. He looked in the direction Nganda had located Lubele and found him still standing there. Just as Kamuyuga's eyes rested on his brother, the messengers who had left Kamuyuga stood before Lubele. Lubele, on his part, fumbled in his *kanzu* and the whole routine was repeated detail by detail. A little while later, the team mounted by the messengers marched up the road leading to the office of the D.C.

As Lubele began to recover, he was standing face to face with Kamuyuga. He was greatly struck; his face brightened wholly. Their hands shook in a tight grip, and their eyes were engaged in a communication more efficient than their tongues could do.

"Are you well?"

"Aaah, just as you see us. We are all well."

"I have been talking to your wife over there." Kamuyuga turned round and pointed at the cluster of women amongst which Nganda sat.

"Ooh, yes. We came together in the morning. I had bananas and I have by now sold all of them away."

"Are you preparing to leave now?"

"Not immediately. I have done with everything. Now I still have to buy a hoe. But the Indian shop-owner has closed down." Lubele spoke in a low voice, mixing Swahili with vernacular.

"Which shop?"

"The one at the corner. I'll have to wait a little. They say that the Indian is taking his lunch, but it is three hours since he closed up."

"Then I'll be ahead of you, because I feel hungry and very tired."

"By the way, did you leave Pwani today?"

"No. We left Pwani two days ago and slept on the way. Yesterday at about three o'clock in the afternoon we reached Mikumi, where we spent the night. This morning we started from Mikumi without stopping anywhere until we came in sight of Bulembe mountains, where we stopped for the driver to see his family at a house somewhere."

"I will make great haste. Once the Indian opens his shop, I will buy and start for home at once."

Lubele bent his stiff backbone and fished out some I bananas which lay in his basket. Four bananas. He stretched up again and handed them to Kamuyuga.

"These ones were not bought. The only ones."

"Aaah, they are quite enough. Let me leave you now. I will walk slowly and you will catch up with me on the way."

Kamuyuga started, passing by the group where Nganda sat. He lifted his *kanzu* and brought out a ten-cent coin. He gave it to a woman sitting opposite Nganda and picked ten huge, ripe bananas. Then saying goodbye to Nganda, he left the market place, heading southwards, his basket clasped under his armpit. He fished out one banana and peeled it. He ate the banana as he walked, feeling acutely the pain that was registered by the soles of his feet as he took the footpath leading out of the little town.

The morning sun poured her radiance over the chilled village of Mpunguta. Dew lay on the wilting grass, the tree leaves, the grass-thatched roofs, on the bare red earth of the dense network of footpaths that ran winding in the bush like long snakes. The dew drops, like grains of sand, glittered in the faint morning rays, dazzling the eyes of early-risers. There was every sign of another sunny, hot day. The wind blew lightly, its bulk of very humid air extracting little from the dew that glimmered all over the exposed earth. Far in the horizon, the Mpunguta hills, with their bare rocks here and there, looked like tiny pimples on the skin of a scabies sufferer. The whole plain was long awake. Smoke creeped along the twisted vents and finally rose up skywards in unstable wriggles from patches in the grass thatch on the isolated homesteads.

The news of the return of Kamuyuga had spread like an epidemic all over Mpunguta, Nlimanja and the nearby Anyalungu villages. Everybody had grown eager to see him, to see what Pwani could make of a person, to hear of their sons and relatives about whom they had gone without news for long periods of time.

As the sun grew hotter and hotter, the compound of Kamuyuga became more and more filled. People sat around Kamuyuga. He had put on new clothes a - white *kanzu* over khaki trousers and brand-new, black, plastic shoes. He looked very happy. Immediately to his right sat Lubele, who kept smiling and advocating all that Kamuyuga narrated. The two sons of Kamuyuga, Zaleme and

Mashaka, kept standing far off the scene, watching their father admiringly, as he was the sole speaker of the gathering. Their eyes did not part with the bright, new clothes Kamuyuga wore. Kamuyuga, as the subject of interest, made the presence of other people shadowy. There were Muyeya, Mbembela, Kadufi, Mulenge and many other Anyalungu elders. There were also people who came from as far off as Mkolomo. They kept their heads raised and their eyes permanently fixed on Kamuyuga.

There were a lot of interruptions to the tales Kamuyuga told. Now and again, there was a new arrival and Kamuyuga had to break and respond to a greeting, many times with a shake of hands.

The tales Kamuyuga related had neither beginning nor end. He explained one thing in answer to a question, and another, in explanation to a still different query. Naturally some people's questions never got answers, however many times they were put forth. Frequently Lubele bent this way and that, and in little more than a whisper, briefly explained something or other, but very obliquely, to an enthusiast whose confusion Kamuyuga had never bothered to clear.

He spoke of the beauties he had seen, the success of the people at Pwani, the strictness of the D.C. of Pwani and many other things.

"People know how to make money there. Not like this land, drinking and hunting *twichi* and nothing else," he said, shaking his head. His audience listened as if it was their first time to hear such talk about Pwani. It seemed to somewhat overcome them, but they struggled to shake off this conviction and give themselves to the scope of their daily realities.

The questions became fewer and fewer. The arrivals, too, became fewer than departures and by noon all the neighbours had dispersed. Lubele remained.

"Did you get greetings from me when you were at Pwani?"

"Who did you send the greetings with?"

"Binda."

"Binda? Which Binda?"

"Binda of Mkomolo."

"In all the years I have been away, I have never come face to face with him. I only heard that he went to Pwani but never saw him in person."

"So it is to him I gave the greetings."

"I never received them."

"And did you hear of the death of Mamkanga?"

"No. Is Mamkanga dead?" "Yes. Three years ago."

"How was it?"

Lubele cleared his throat and swung back his neck to send the grey, slippery sputum flying and landing upon the loose red soil. He leaned against the wall.

"Do you remember that he was working for a certain Indian in the town?"

"I remember it very well."

"So it happened one day that he came up to Mpunguta. I don't know what he came for. By the way, did you know a certain messenger called Ncholoka?"

"Ncholoka ... no. I never knew him."

"It was this..." Lubele jumped in his seat. "I have remembered it all now."

"When Mamkanga was living in the town working for his Indian, that messenger of the D.C., Ncholoka, used to come here and sleep with the younger wife of Mamkanga, daily."

"Did Mamkanga not live with a wife in town?"

"He had his elder wife in Majengo. He used to live with them in turn. He would take one wife to Majengo for one week, and the next week another wife. Now, as some people say, Ncholoka slept with both those wives without them knowing that he did it to both of them. So on that day it was with the younger wife."

"And how did Mamkanga come to know?"

"It is all a long story. This Ncholoka had a friend who was also a messenger of the D.C. They used to go along together all the time. Then, one day, they met the wives of Mamkanga at his house here at Mpunguta, when they were looking for people who had not paid their taxes. Mamkanga himself had not paid the tax so he had gone to hide in the bush. Then Ncholoka and his friend wanted the women. From then I don't know what happened exactly, but all that people know is that both wives loved Ncholoka. So Ncholoka tricked his colleague. He arranged it so that he could enjoy both of them without considering his colleague, who had informed on him."

Kamuyuga smiled broadly with apparent enlightenment.

"So Mamkanga came here one day."

"Eeeh Kamuyuga yelled.

"He met Ncholoka on the bed, and stabbed him with a knife."

"Did he die?"

"Why not? He died on the path to town as he tried to escape."

As Lubele finished saying this, Mugindi came out and laid a tray of food before her husband and Lubele. They continued talking as they ate.

"I was then at my home at Nlimanja, sometime in the afternoon, when I heard cries from the bush. A man was yelling for help, very desperately. I ran there, knife in hand. Several of us who had heard the cries ran there to see who it was."

"And who was it?"

"It was himself — Mamkanga."

"Was he alone?"

"Yes."

"What was he doing?"

"He was only standing under a tree, crying. His neck was very dark. He had been trying to hang himself."

"And why was the neck dark?" The eyes of Kamuyuga seemed to come out of their sockets with fascination.

"Heee! Bark rope. It was the rope that made his neck dark. The rope was very weak and it broke off. Thus he dropped from the branch."

"I can't understand this. Why did he cry for help?"

"He said that he didn't want to play with his life anymore. He cried, 'No! No! No!, I don't want to die. It is terrible I don't like it!'"

Kamuyuga felt like bursting out in loud laugh, but instead the laugh ended up in a pitiful smile.

Lubele continued. "I took my knife and cut the loop off his neck and we escorted him to his home. But the messengers and the police came to fetch him, that very afternoon."

"And what happened then?"

"They hanged him," Lubele said in a sad tone, turning his eyes away.

THREE

That evening, Lubele went to bed very early. For a long time he kept looking at the roof as if his thoughts were all spread out on the thatch. He recalled things, those which were hidden under their black nature and others under the great heap called Time; things which he saw happen and those passed on to him by others. He thought about the bravery of that great Anyalungu Chief, Njunju, about his ancestry which somehow was linked with that of Kamuyuga. There was nobody who could confirm the fact that the father of Kamuyuga, Kahocho, and his own father, Ndandanga, were cousins.

However, there was one thing he was sure of. His father and the father of Kamuyuga were hanged by the Germany on the same day. It was very long ago. He was told this by his mother. He was then about three years old, and Kamuyuga was two, when their fathers ceased to live.

That particular deed which had taken place outside the office of the German D.C. had united Lubele and Kamuyuga. Lubele never knew what his father looked like. Perhaps he resembled that celebrated Anyalungu chief, Njunju. Perhaps.

One day, when still a young boy, Lubele asked his mother, "Where did Father go?"

His mother tried to look away and evade that heart-piercing question each time. The still-young Lubele, clothed in black, tattered calico, continued persistently. "Where did he go, Mother?"

His mother wouldn't say anything but scolded him and for a time the boy left the question aside.

Another day when playing with some other children, one of them, called Muyeya, said defiantly to Lubele, "Your father was hanged. It was because of, big-headedness. If you want to be as big-headed as your father, try for yourself."

The words thrashed acutely the heart of the young boy. He didn't, however, mind the insult but concerned himself with the fate of his father, which had now to come to light. The other boys turned to Muyeya curiously.

"Who told you this?" Lubele asked indignantly.

"I heard it yesterday. My mother mentioned this when she was talking to Father," Muyeya replied, with a pride that oppressed heavily the heart of Lubele.

Another boy, who himself died three years later, asked, "How? Hanging how? What do they mean by hanging?" The boys looked at each other and then turned their eyes to Muyeya, the source of the sad narrative.

"Even I myself do not know. They say that he hung."

"Maybe hanging like a mango," another boy had suggested, pointing at a mango hanging on its stalk in a tree some distance away. All of them gazed at the mango for a while without saying anything. They found it horrible and abandoned the whole topic completely.

But Lubele had not left the matter alone. That evening he asked his mother again about his father, but this time his question was modified.

"What do they mean by hanging?

"What?" his mother had asked him, in a voice that showed temper.

"They say Father was hanged. How?"

His mother, without asking who told him so, just let out the story that day. She did not have the aura of sadness about her as she did the other times. Instead she remembered Ndandanga, her late husband.

"Yes, he died," she answered.

"And who killed him?"

"The Europeans, the Germans."

"Why did they do it?" This question seemed to have no answer. Lubele's mother looked up for a while, biting her finger and swallowing. But it was to come out at length.

"They killed him because they wanted me. Your father was enraged so much that he wanted to kill them, one of them. So they said he was a killer. The father of Kamuyuga, too. But him for some other reason. He ran away from one of the European who had made him a slave." She said these words as much to herself as to her son, her eyes fixed steadfast on the moon of the evening, as though what she said had been written on it.

Whenever Lubele remembered his father, Ndandanga, he saw a mango in his mind's eye. It hung on its long stem. That was the symbol of his father. It was a big mango which had eyes, ears and everything like a human face. It was a tender face, hanging without saying anything, day after day. As he grew older, Lubele's symbol of his hanged father changed. He saw him oscillate on rockers. Ndandanga would rock with a sad smile at first, then the oscillations would become faster and faster and he would laugh a wild laugh. Finally he would rock so fast that his figure spread all over between the two peaks of oscillation, crying very desperately, and the features would fade from his face.

When Lubele heard that Kahocho, the father of Kamuyuga, hung by the side of Ndandanga, the hanging mango then stood for Kahocho and the rocking fellow for Ndandanga. Thus for all his life that was the way Lubele pictured and remembered his parent.

The two sons, Lubele and Kamuyuga, had lived together till adulthood as brothers. Their old mothers had died before they had even married and thus they became sole guardians of themselves. They had remembered their parents together once every year. A white, bearded he-goat was slaughtered at the graveyard site to let the blood soak and some beer was poured for the fore-forefathers to drink. Prayers were sent to them now and again, reminding them not to forget the difficulties of the world, that they should bestow their offspring with their goodwill, and that they should remit their indulgences.

Lubele then drew his thoughts forward from the past, changing them to another line. He thought of the new manners of Kamuyuga, somewhat like the town Swahilis. Was he going to turn a Swahili? Kamuyuga spoke Swahili most of the time and very fluently. He thought of the two sons of Kamuyuga, Zaleme and Mashaka, how they had lived for many years in the absence of their father. He thought of the hunting in the bush, and the skill of the dog, Fukara. He remembered when the other dog, Kalibukufa, had caught a *twichi* and ate by himself. His elder son, Lunja, had tried to run after the dog to save the meat, but Kalibukufa had run away to eat the *twichi* by himself. He hated that dog and one day had almost decided to kill it.

The room grew darker and darker and the vision of Lubele suddenly fell under the bar of darkness. He tilted his head and caught sight of the dim flame as it went out by two lifeless wriggles.

"There is no oil," Nganda, who was sleeping on a mat below, informed her husband. She stretched out her arm to fetch the empty tin and shook it. The sharp ringing of a few sand grains told the whole truth. The room fell in complete darkness and eyes became useless organs. Still the husband and wife could feel the presence of each other. They talked in low voices with several breaks of silence.

"Tomorrow start preparing beer for a sacrifice."

"Another sacrifice this year?" Nganda wondered.

"For the arrival of Kamuyuga. Eight years is not a short period."

The next afternoon Kamuyuga descended the hill from Mpunguta towards the river Mfele. Behind him his son Zaleme followed. Kamuyuga was full of thought and took much time to shift his steps forward. His eyes wandered here and there, wherever the sun's light fell, looking at each point very carefully.

Much of it was the same. He reached the river Mfele and stood on a rock by its side. The river flowed very smoothly under the shade of two tall trees that made a thick canopy above. The water was very clear, showing everything that lay at the bottom. He stepped on the bridge and faced the upper side of the river. Behind him a huge rock projected from the water cutting the river waters into halves. The halves reunited on the other side of the rock, where the water sang two notes, one high, the other low. These, bass and tenor, were woven up by the current and sung the old song of the valley. It was a familiar song to anybody who belonged to either Mpunguta or Nlimanja. And Kamuyuga, too, recognized it. It reminded him of his past life in the village and told him that he was back to the right place where he belonged, that he was never lost. He stood there for a while longer.

The river continued to sing on and on.Probably the water knew many things, secret things, he thought, and he sensed that it opened up many things before him. Would it open up his future, too, he wondered. Was there success in his plans, the plans he had in all his dreams when at Pwani? He listened more and more carefully but the river seemed unsure, and seemed to sing without pattern. Kamuyuga left the river to itself and ascended up the hill to Nlimanja. Zaleme came behind him walking leisurely, deep in his own cogitations.

The family of Lubele was at home. They had been expecting Kamuyuga as he had promised them the day before. Lubele surrendered his stool to Kamuyuga and seated himself on a grinding-stone. They greeted each other, Kamuyuga not showing much cheerfulness. Lubele tried to introduce one topic after another but he found that it was he alone who talked, and at last he chose to wait for his neighbour to talk. Then Kamuyuga looked up slowly and his face brightened as a day-dreamer's does after a prolonged period of absent-mindedness.

"Where is my daughter Dayela?" Kamuyuga asked, referring in the familiar way to his kinsman's daughter. "I have not seen her since my arrival."

"Don't you know? She was married three years ago." "Married? It is my first time to hear this. To whom is she married?"

"She is married to Zayumba."

"Zayumba? I don't think that I know this Zayumba."

"Son of Chochocho of Mkomolo. Have you forgotten Chochocho?"

"Had he a son called Zayumba?"

"Haaa! That's only a nickname. His name —"

"Yusefu," Nganda gave the clue. "That is his Christian name. But people know only this other one — Zayumba."

"I think I saw him the day before yesterday." Kamuyuga said, trying to recall.

"Did you recognize him?" Nganda and Lubele said in unison.

"No, it was he who recognized me. When I left for Pwani he was only a boy."

"And where did you see him?"

"It was there in the town."

"That boy does not stay at home. That boy, I tell you he is very different. He cannot live without money. Other boys, aah! Like these sons I have got, only hunting *twichi* in the bush. Will they dress the *twichi?*" Nganda barked this last at her elder son, Lunja.

"When Binda of Mkomolo said he was going to Pwani, I told him to convey my greetings to you. I thought that he had told you of the marriage of Dayela, too."

"No, Binda didn't, for we never met. And what was the bride price?" Kamuyuga did not fail to enquire.

"Aaah," Lubele uttered, feeling the words not ready to come out. "Some five, six goats and that —"

"Haaa! Didn't Chochocho give money?"

"Some sixty shillings. We said that the other forty I would receive after the marriage."

"And have you got it?"

"In fact, I have not. Because one day I met this Zayumba in the town. He gave me forty shillings. Then, when I ask his father Chochocho, he says that I have already got my forty shillings. And I say, no, because if it meant the money Zayumba gave me, and then I don't agree with the manner I received that money. It was not the manner people give money that has to do with bride price. That money, Zayumba gave me just as a present."

"True," Kamuyuga advocated. "How is this Chochocho? Does he want to show that he is not aware of the manners of the tribe? He was born at Mkomolo, and has lived there all his life. If he had been somewhere else, we would say that he has been contaminated." For a while after he spoke, no one said anything.

"I want to start up a business," Kamuyuga broke into the silence.

"What business?"

"I don't have a particular type in mind right now.

Something of a shop or the like."

"Mmh, here at Mpunguta or where?"

"Eeeh. But I will need money," Kamuyuga said, looking down and swinging his legs side-ways. "How many goats do you have up to now?" Kamuyuga continued after an interval of silence.

"Not many left. You know the problems one always has with such property. Several rites need goats, sometimes very unexpectedly. Two weeks ago, Lunja went to herd the animals and as he was coming back home, two policemen passed here. The first thing they spoke to me was tax, as usual. When they saw that I had the chits, one of them insisted to have the big he-goat, Dudu. 'We are very tired', they said, 'and because it is already dark you can't cook food for us. Maybe give us this goat.' And Dudu went away just like that."

As they talked thus, Lunja appeared with the animals. The attention of Lubele, and particularly Kamuyuga, was focused on the goats. Their stomachs had swollen greatly, but they still bent their necks this way and that to pick some leaf or whatever they could eat.

"What about this goat, this huge one?" Kamuyuga enquired.

"Which, Zimba? This is Zimba, the biggest he-goat left with me. And it won't live long, for I will slaughter it for the sacrifice."

"You have had no sacrifice recently? I thought that it must have passed."

"We have had one, but this is for you. No doubt you have had no sacrifices when in Pwani."

Kamuyuga did not answer. He seemed bored. "I want this big goat, this Zimba. It has to stay with me for a while. You know that my pen has only she-goats. I want this one to amount the females."

Kamuyuga looked at Lubele full in the face, and seemed to trace the words as they slowly sank down into the head of his friend. Lubele thought hard. He knew that he could not resist this request. He yielded.

Two days later, Lubele passed at the house of Kamuyuga on his way from the market. Kamuyuga was quite busy.

Lubele halted and put down the empty basket. Lunja, who had accompanied him, put down his, too. The place was very dusty. Kamuyuga, who was dressed in tattered khaki trousers, was dusty all over. His back and upper body were naked and dust adhered to the sticky, sweaty skin.

"What are you planning to do?" Lubele asked.

"My house had only a single door, you know."

"And what is a front door for?"

"This will be a shop. You remember I talked to you the other day."

"Yes I remember."

"So is it. I will also have to break two windows. One each side. You know this house I built before going to Pwani. It had no windows either. I hate a house that harbours darkness during day. It looks much like a grave."

"Just like my poor house," Lubele said shyly.

"Nearly so."

Kamuyuga went on working on the wall for a while before he said anything more. "Let me find you a stool." "No, I won't stay long. I feel exhausted."

"I have something to tell you. Or rather to ask you."

"Just say it," Lubele said, and, turning round, he hoisted the empty basket and gave it to Lunja. "Go ahead, Lunja. I am coming." Lunja took the two baskets and proceeded home.

"How are these people? Are they really good people? What is your opinion of them?"

"Who are those?"

"Muyeya, Mulenge and others."

"In what thing?"

"You remember the other day I told you that I need money for this business I want to establish. So I approached these people." Kamuyuga paused and looked questioningly at Lubele. "I had myself about fifty shillings I happened to save when I was at

Pwani. Mulenge has given me ten shillings. At first he refused. Not completely, but he showed signs of unwillingness. He went into his house and a few minutes later a discussion with his wife started. I had expected this when I saw him enter the house so I ran to the wall and listened. "Give him. He is a good man," the wife spoke of me. Mulenge himself did not say anything. His wife kept imploring him for a long while before Mulenge came out and handed me ten shillings. And if I was used to going to his house or if I had been here all the time, Mulenge would have thought that I had relations with his wife because she pressed upon her husband so much."

Lubele kept his eyes to the ground without saying a word. He seemed more to be thinking of some other thing than listening to Kamuyuga.

Kamuyuga continued, "*Mzee* Muyeya has given me five shillings. I know that such old people save a lot of money. But they are very stingy. I went to his house yesterday evening. I implored him to lend me the money for quite long. At last he went in and brought me only five shillings. And as for Kadufi, he refused me straightaway and I didn't waste much time with him."

Kamuyuga stopped narrating and waited for Lubele to speak. Lubele kept his silence. Kamuyuga continued. "One thing I will tell you. At Pwani, the Swahilis call it *kuungishana*. This one lends aid to that, and that one lends to this. That's why they succeed. I found the money not enough and I'm sorry to say I will have to sell that he-goat you gave me."

"Why?" Lubele spoke for the first time, his whole body showing alarm.

"Because I have not got enough money."

"I will give you the price of that goat. But please, that goat you should not sell. It is for the sacrifice, do you forget?"

"Sacrifices do a lot of damage. I think that since you have had your sacrifice, I can only wait to have it next time you have another."

The eyes of Lubele flashed. The words seemed to have struck him so much that he could not wish to speak again on the subject.

"Anyway I will take the price of the goat. Give it to me," said Kamuyuga.

"Tomorrow."

"Why tomorrow? I know that you have the money here with you, sewn around your waist. Why do you people want to twist matters so much!"

"Where I keep my money does not matter. You will get it tomorrow."

The next day, early in the morning, Kamuyuga was at the door of Lubele. He received twenty shillings. That amount was not the price of the goat, of course. But Kamuyuga wouldn't let Lubele give him less at a time when he knew that a lot of shilling coins were buried under Lubele's bed, leaving aside those on his body.

As soon as he reached home, Kamuyuga fetched the goat and proceeded into the town. He was not there long before a servant from an Indian shop came running after him and handed him ten shillings.

FOUR

The rains had come round again. No more time for idle gatherings,
no more time for much drinking. Women turned the rice fields
their new homes, where they stayed the whole day long. They
always worked from dawn to dusk, with everybody complaining
of shortage of time. Men seemed to have nothing to do in particular.
They had, in fact, everything before them, and all to be accomplished
in that single season.

There was the tilling of maize fields, the weeding of plantains,
the only crop that yielded immediate cash at the market place.
There was the yearly adding of thatch to the roofs which, day after
day, were found to seep water, wetting everything inside. Everybody
looked as though he had just come home from a long journey
only to find all that mess awaiting him.

The rain had just started to shower on one such day. The wife of Kamuyuga, Mugindi, was seated behind a table in the little shop. She kept her eyes cast outside, watching the thick, light-brown sheet that flowed to fill the river Mfele below. The door had remained open for the whole day. She had been there shelling groundnuts after sweeping the whole house. None of these tasks was actually the reason for her presence at home. She had been there to serve her customers.

For two days, then, nobody had come to the shop. She was very bored and wished that somebody would relieve her.

That year she had not prepared her rice fields. Her husband, Kamuyuga, was the real cause. The shop was another. Kamuyuga had fascinated her with his ambitions, which after a time became hers, too: the servants, they would employ to till the fields; servants to wash her clothing, fetch water for her, and do all her housework; that she would sit knitting with her legs stretched out on a clean mat, just like the Bulembe Indian women did. But now she foresaw a shaky future and doubt came to her. Andunje, whom they had employed to till the maize field, had not yet got his five shillings. She was worried. The heap of unshelled groundnuts fell lower and lower each time and she continued shelling absent-mindedly.

It rained thus for two solid hours before the rain came to a sudden stop. Mist towered all over the damp air. Mugindi turned round in her chair. She pushed the door behind her a bit wider open and peered through. Kamuyuga lay there as still as ever. Her eyes remained fixed, perusing the folds of the brown cotton blanket sprawled over him. Then she jerked herself upright and proceeded into the room. The earth floor had become muddy. She looked up at the grass roof. It was all wet, water everywhere. She turned her sight down again and eyed Kamuyuga on the bed. The blanket was partly wet.

Kamuyuga opened his eyes and looked fixedly at his wife. No part of his body moved.

"How are you now?"

"No better," Kamuyuga replied in little more than a whisper, after a strong effort to gather his consciousness. He had become very thin, his cheek bones sticking out sharply.

"How, then? Should I go and call Lubele?"

"No."

Mugindi looked disappointed. She did not understand what he was thinking about. How then could she, a woman, manage this alone? There was nobody in the house. The sons, Zaleme and Mashaka, were not at home. She went out of the room and opened the back door. It was all very wet and damp. And there too in the backyard, she could see the firewood. It was all wet. She had forgotten it in the open. She ran into the kitchen and brought out a tiny pot.

"Take this." She gave Kamuyuga the juice of some herbs in a cup. Kamuyuga shook his head lightly. He was shivering. Sweat poured from his whole body, soaking the blanket and the sheets below. Mugindi stood bewildered. She did not know what to do next. Kamuyuga heaved heavy sighs. He pulled himself up and vomited huge balls of *ugali* mixed with blood. Some of the bloody stuff gushed through his nose. He vomited for a time and then it subsided. His eyes lost all sign of life and he fixed them blankly on the roof.

Mugindi put down the cup of herbs, closed the two doors of the house and rushed along the little path leading to the river and across to Nlimanja. She stopped several times on the way, hesitatingly, her heart thumping hard.

"Mamaa . . ." a voice came from Nlimanja. It was Simon's high-pitched voice, producing echoes in the valley.

"Qui-i-ck, shemeji should rush here. It is urgent, you hear?"

"Eeee ... ?" Simon returned, claiming to have not caught her.

"Shenzi . . . You keep teasing. I say tell your father to come quickly!"

A final "Eeee . . ." was heard, showing that she was understood. She rushed back home.

Fifteen minutes later Lubele arrived. His legs were all muddy and wet. He went into the room. Kamuyuga still lay motionless. Mugindi stood at Lubele's side, shaking all over. They stood silently, looking at the pool of blood without saying a thing. After thinking for ten minutes in total silence, Lubele said, "Bring five shillings."

"We don't have any. There is no money in the whole house. There is no business. You know of the jealousy of the people of Mpunguta. They envy my husband. They prefer going to get their things in town to buying things from this shop."

Lubele stepped out of the bedroom and into the shop. Mugindi trailed behind him. They stopped in the shop.

"Look," Mugindi pointed out to Lubele, "what you see here is the first stock we ever brought from Bulembe and yet it is not finished," she said sadly, looking at the dusty match boxes lying on a shelf.

"Alright. I will come again. Take care of him," Lubele said as he made his way out.

Muyeya was sitting at the fireside in his mud house that evening. The firesticks which were not yet dry resisted burning and released smoke that filled the small ante-room. Muyeya sat facing Lubele, their hands and knees almost aching as they crouched near the hearth. Muyeya had a gloomy air about him, and there had been little talk since the arrival of Lubele.

"You have been at home the whole of today?" Lubele broke the silence.

Muyeya did not take it to answer immediately. He turned his face to the right, to evade the thick smoke. The question seemed to get lost and go out with the current of smoke. Muyeya started in the end, his voice showing little expression.

"I have been adding thatch to the roof. There was leakage in this corner."

Lubele did not take much time longer to realize that Muyeya felt uneasy about his presence. He thought it better to plunge directly into what had sent him there.

"I am in a difficulty, a great difficulty. It is about my brother, Kamuyuga. He is very ill, vomiting blood. I seek your help." Here

Lubele broke off to allow for Muyeya's reaction. Muyeya turned his head towards Lubele and in the half-darkness he looked into the eyes of his visitor.

"Of what help can I be to you in this affair?"

"You know what help you are to give. I know that you have done it to him because Kamuyuga has wronged you. I am not myself taking sides with him in this case. But please don't kill him. He is my brother."

Muyeya slid his stool backwards and bent his head to the hearth. He said nothing.

Lubele waited for a reply, but there was none. He chose to continue. "You, Muyeya, and myself have lived together since childhood. You know my character very well. I am violent sometimes but I don't want quarrels or scorn. On my part, too, I know who Muyeya is, your ancestry, besides many other things. Today, this brother of ours, Kamuyuga has just returned from Pwani. His manners have altogether become different. He has taken manners of Pwani to plant them here, many things. I can say it is three months since last he stepped upon Nlimanja, as if he has no kinsman there. But all this I don't mind."

As he finished saying this, Lubele noticed the eyes of the wife of Muyeya peering in their direction from the sleeping-room. She had been asleep but then chose to come and listen. She had stolen into her peeping position very stealthily and was about to sit when Lubele noticed her. Lubele went on.

"Kamuyuga sold my he-goat away, that he-goat, Zimba, without my permission, and I said nothing."

Muyeya, as if pricked by these accusations against Kamuyuga, now came into the conversation in fuller spirits. "Kamuyuga is very proud. He thinks that because he has been to Pwani, then those who are born in Mpunguta and die in Mpunguta without any travelling are mere dung. What does he mean by saying that the people of Mpunguta are very stupid, that they can't even put up a shop, that they keep sewing up coins round their waists and go to sleep feeling them all the nights long? And many other things."

"I have heard all that, I know it all," Lubele pleaded sympathetically.

"I just can't tell all that Kamuyuga has done. He has come from Pwani running away from his creditors. He thinks that we don't know, but do people not travel between Bulembe and Pwani?"

"They do, they do." Lubele felt very shy. He had himself never heard of this and he didn't like to hear it, particularly from a person like Muyeya.

"Binda, this Binda of Mkomolo, met Kamuyuga at Pwani. Kamuyuga was in a very bad state, they say. Creditors all around him. And he could not even take Binda, his kinsman, to his home. Why, do you think? Now Binda has returned and from Binda people hear that Kamuyuga escaped his creditors. That's why he came here." Lubele by then was already feeling much smaller than a baby.

"Those who come from Pwani, leaving aside Binda, say "that Kamuyuga at Pwani was a nobody. A mere *muhuni*. If that is not true, then why did he return as naked as he went? Did he bring anything more than an empty basket, filled with nothing but rags? He didn't even bring new clothes for his wife or sons. Deny this if you think you can!"

"No, no. He didn't bring anything," Lubele answered, feeling harassed.

"Now why does he tell people that he had left his things, at Pwani and that they will one day be brought? Do you, Lubele, think that if Kamuyuga was a man like other Anyalungu we know living there, do you think he would leave his wife here to go about with any man, sleeping with the town messengers, without thinking of coming to fetch her?" Muyeya paused and in the half-darkness he looked at Lubele, who then tried to conquer the humiliation that pressed upon him like a huge granite rock. Muyeya continued.

"But what I am particularly angry with is that Kamuyuga has despised me and completely dishonoured me. He has said that when he approached me to give him something for his capital, I gave him only five shillings. I sent Kadufi last week to tell him to bring that five shillings back. This he hasn't, till this day. And I swear before you that he will bring these five shillings."

"I know it all," Lubele approved sadly.

"No. This Kamuyuga cannot disturb the peace of the village. I am five years older than he. Only that he grows old too quickly and for the pride he has, people over-estimate him."

"Now listen, Muyeya," Lubele began in the tone of accumulated courage. "It is good that you have told me all that Kamuyuga has done to you. And now I have heard the story first-hand. Take these five shillings, and tomorrow I will send Simon to bring a he-goat. Sorry that I wasn't able to bring it with me this evening. This matter you should try to ignore, because among the village elders you are the eldest. Then if you always resort to temper, you will lose the faith we all have in you." Lubele finished these words and a gap of silence ensued.

Muyeya only looked down. Then Lubele poured before him a heap of the rounded coins with holes in their centre. A heap of them. They gave a distinct smell of the red Nlimanja earth. He counted them before Muyeya. Ten of them one shilling. Twenty, thirty, forty, fifty. They made up the exact sum, five shillings.

Muyeya received them in his hands and supported his bulky palms on his lap. From then onwards there was not much dialogue, or more precisely, there was one, altogether complex. They understood each other in the writings each read in the eyes of his colleague. It was settled.

FIVE

For three days it had continued to rain in the same manner. Nobody went out to work. The sun, too, never came out until late in the afternoons. Mist lay here and there over the Mpunguta hills in the distance. However, Lubele had managed to check on the improvement of Kamuyuga's health. Every day he crossed the valley over to Mpunguta at least twice. Nganda would walk behind him carrying a basket of foodstuffs.

The fourth day started off totally different. It dawned with the brightening of the whole eastern horizon, and lastly the king of the stars fired up brightly into the blue heavens. Lubele did not go out into the fields. That rain which had showered for three days consecutively had conquered the resistance of the thatch on his house. His son, Lunja, helped him hoist the bundles of elephant grass from where they lay in a huge pile a distance away. They worked diligently for hours.

At about two in the afternoon, Nganda appeared carrying a gourd of water which she balanced elegantly on her head. Her legs were dirty with the mud of the rice fields. It was quite hot and Lubele, after being satisfied with the work, decided to take a rest.

The father and son sat under the shade of a mango tree in the compound. They talked little. Lubele looked hard at Lunja. Lunja was growing into a man, he thought. He noticed the tough, firm muscles of the thighs. What year was he born? He thought harder. He knew that he could not remember the precise year. Quite long ago. That year he had a quarrel with Nganda. She was then pregnant, carrying this very child, Lunja. He had sent her to her parents at Mkomolo. It was at the time people spoke of the great war. That war, he had been urged to join the army, and with this too he recalled that big-eyed *jumbe* who kept persuading and actually threatening him on the subject day after day. But now he was dead.

Lubele kept wandering far and near in his thoughts until he was interrupted by the appearance of Kamuyuga. Kamuyuga approached in feeble steps, pushing himself forward stiffly and seated himself on a stool Lunja brought from the kitchen.

"How do you feel today? I wasn't able to come this morning," Lubele enquired with his usual air of concern.

"Just don't worry about coming to Mpunguta. I feel much better now. I could as well say that I have recovered."

As Kamuyuga finished saying this, Simon, the younger son of Lubele, came out of the kitchen sagging under the weight of a tray of food, and laid it before his father. They encircled it and began to eat.

"You said that you would close down the shop, now what about the stock? What will you do with it?" Lubele asked as they ate. Kamuyuga swallowed the lump of *ugali* a bit unchewed as he hurried to take up the question.

"I know what I will do with it. I can sell it to some shop-owners in the town if I fail in my plans."

"And what are your plans?"

"I want to leave this place as I told you the other day. Then I will shift the shop to where I will go."

"Do you want to go back to Pwani?"

"Pwani could be one of the places. But I would like to go to . . ." Kamuyuga could not finish; as a lump of *ugali* made its way into his mouth. He pointed beyond the Mpunguta hills.

"Where, to Mkomolo?"

Kamuyuga nodded in assent. "But I have not made my final decision yet. Mugindi insists upon staying in Mpunguta. These women, I just can't say what they actually are. She speaks of 'our land'. Is there no land at Mkomolo? Do people there build houses in the air?"

They continued to eat in silence. The bowl of *ajuni* emptied and Simon stood up to go and refill it. Meanwhile the little group sat up on their stools, their fingers pounding the white lumps of *ugali* held in their right hands. They continued talking.

"But if you really mean to go to Mkomolo, you will really be far from the town. And if it is carrying bananas on the head to market, your head will grow bald. Look at the wife of Mulenge."

"But that one is natural."

"Natural? Do women grow bald? It is because of heavy loads, bananas!"

"Yes, that's true, I agree. I have tried to consider this but I just can't think of seeing that snake. Muyeya? No. I shouldn't set my eyes upon him."

The last lump cleared off the bowl and Simon hoisted the tray back to the kitchen. For fifteen minutes they sat without talking. Silence reigned in that midday sun until a new person came into sight.

"*Hodii . . .*"

"*Karibu,*" Lubele returned, in the most hospitable and gracious tone he could manage with his ever-coarse voice.

The man approached. He was a tall, slender, middle-aged man, dressed after the fashion of the town Swahilis. He cast his eyes this side and that, and seemed to depend much upon a stick, with which he dug holes in the wet soil in front of him, for seeing the path. Lubele gave his stool to him.

"Lunja," Lubele called, "bring that high chair." A moment later the high chair was erected for the visitor.

"*Alhamdulillahi,*" the stranger murmured. "May I have some water to drink?" Lunja stood up again and went to fetch the water.

"Aah, Bwana Saidi, are you well?" Lubele greeted.

"Ah! Just as Allah leads us. Today this, tomorrow that. Thus days pass until one day you go into the grave. I see that the soil is totally wet in all these areas. Much rain, eh?"

"All these days except today. Heavy rains, making us stay indoors."

"*Alhamdulillahi.* We in town only have scattered showers. No actual rain."

"We are near the hills. That's why,"

"Ah! It is the way Allah arranges privileges. It doesn't depend upon hills or what. Today he favours this, tomorrow that."

The water was brought and he drank it by three huge gulps that thundered, seeming to produce explosions at the throat.

"*Allahu Akbaru,*" he said to himself as he handed the empty cup back to Lunja.

"Lunja, go and tell your mother to prepare another meal for a visitor," Lubele whispered to his son. Lunja stood up and went into the kitchen.

"The sun is really hot today, eh? I am sweating all over."

"Have you been very far anyway?" Lubele asked Saidi.

"I started off at the first cock-crow. I passed here at about seven, climbed the hills and down to the other side."

"Where, to Mkomolo?"

Ah! Mkomolo here? I have been to Ngenge today!"

"You really walk. It is not possible to imagine you town folk being able to walk so much."

"Me? I went to the war, and not a mere town idler. Didn't you know that?"

"Ah! this I knew," Lubele said, nodding his head. Simon came out and announced that the meal was ready.

"Lead the guest to his meal, Simon," Lubele instructed his son.

"Allahu Akbaru," Saidi murmured for another time as he stood up and went into the house. Kamuyuga, who had seemed to feel uneasy with the presence of Saidi, then seemed to recover and he assumed a better mood.

"I seem to forget who this Saidi is," Kamuyuga asked in a low voice.

"Don't you know Saidi-wa-Manamba of Mshenye? Truly?"

"Saidi-wa-Manamba?" Kamuyuga sank into recollection.

"Do you know that Greek called Geregoli?"

"That agent of *manamba?*"

"Yes, that old Greek with scabies on his arms."

"And what about those scabies? Can he not get rid of them?"

"Hmm! He seems to have been bewitched. Not ordinary scabies."

"And what did you want to say about him?"

"So this Saidi is under Geregoli. He goes out to speak to people in the village urging them to enroll in the *manamba.*"

"Ah, yes. Now I recall this Saidi. But is he old so soon?"

"It is him, Saidi-wa-Manamba. He has been doing this job since after the war. And as you see him now, it must be that a Greek needs *manamba* somewhere."

"And how much is he paid?"

"Oooh! quite highly. That Geregoli, I hear he gets five shillings for every head he successfully enrols. As for Saidi, it must be between one and two shillings per head."

Kamuyuga was thoughtful, apparently reckoning the pay.

"How did Saidi come to get this job?"

"I don't know matters of these town Swahilis. They are very clever."

The stick of Saidi was heard tutting on the ground and he reappeared. He seated himself on the chair.

"Loo, *Alhamdulillahi*. I was very hungry. And now for the remaining distance, I will push myself slowly to arrive at sunset," he said.

Lunja came and sat under the shade unnoticed. Then the keen eyes of Saidi caught a glance of him. He turned his towards the son of Lubele and his little eyes turned in their sockets examining him very carefully.

"Young man," he said to him at length, after giving him a careful eye, "what is your name?"

Lunja, instead of replying, gave a broad, childish smile.

"Lunja, he is called," his father answered for him.

"Did you say, Lunja?" Saidi asked, with apparent zest in his voice.

"Yes, Lunia."

"How about you, Lunja. Can't you go and take up a job at Pwani? Eh! Young man. You ought not to stay at home idling like a child. Come on! You have got to travel and see the world." Then

Saidi looked at the faces of Lubele and Kamuyuga appealingly for their opinion.

Lunja looked down, his hands busy playing shyly with his big toe. He tilted his head this way and that. A strong urge to say "yes" overcame his whole person. His face brightened and Saidi, a skilled professional labour recruiter, could not fail to grasp what his next move should be.

"Alright. Your name is Lunja. Monday after the next one, *manamba* depart for Pwani. So you will have to come this Monday to the house of Gregori. Don't you know the house?"

"Aaa . . . why, he knows it," his father hastened to answer.

"And in Pwani, which Greek this time?" Lubele asked.

"A new Greek. Not a new Greek to this country or to Tanga, but only that he has never taken *manamba* from this area before."

Saidi-wa-Manamba jerked himself up with the help of his stick and got to his feet. Lubele stood up to escort him.

"Is that young man your son?"

"Yes, he is. And also the younger one, Simon, whom you saw there too. But Simon is schooling."

"Where?"

"At Mpunguta school. That mud school at the foot of the Mpunguta hills."

"Mmm . . ." Saidi grunted. "These days someone schooling up to standard four cannot so easily get a job in an office. If it is standard six, then alright. Or at least standard five."

Lubele answered, after appearing to have thought deeply, "I have been planning that at least one of -my sons should get education. Simon should go beyond standard four."

"Where do you think he can get a place? The only middle school is at Mbazala Mission. And nobody can get a place there unless he becomes known to the priests. As for us Muslims, such a chance for our children is what we cannot even dream of."

Lubele examined his situation a bit more carefully than he had done before. He was neither a Muslim like Saidi-wa-Manamba nor was he one dear to the priests.

Saidi continued. "This Lunja, does he go to school, too?"

"No. Ah, this one is only staying at home."

"Don't let him stay at home like that. Urge him to take up this opportunity which has thrown itself at his feet."

"But can Geregoli agree to take him? He is, I thought, a bit too young," said Lubele anxiously.

"Who do you think Gregori is to refuse me?" Saidi said firmly, slightly turning back to face Lubele. "You don't worry! Rely upon me."

Lubele did not escort the visitor further. They shook hands and parted.

SIX

The afternoons in the months of November were always sunny and the sky would always be filled with a lot of smoke from the burning bushes hunters set alight.

In the mornings people were engaged in the preparation of *shambas* for the coming rainy season. Men were engaged in preparing virgin land for the coming year. They pruned bushes and branches of the tall *miombo* trees to allow the sun's rays to reach the growing plants beneath. For such work, one usually asked neighbours to give a hand. A man's wife would brew beer, not much beer usually. Two or three huge pots would do sufficiently. He would then inform the neighbours, fix the day, and they on their part would all come and work in his *shamba*.

On one such day, about five years after the return of Kamuyuga from Pwani, this aspect of village life was in full swing, in the plots of Lubele. From early in the morning, a handful of men felled the branches like monkeys, with skill built up during many years that they and their fathers had done the same thing.

Nobody could talk and be heard. Besides, there was nobody prepared to. The air was filled with the thundering of axes and falling branches. Men whistled and sang softly. Women, on their part gathered in the previous year's plots, weeding. They sang melodiously, blending their high-pitched tones with the few baritone some of them could manage. With that much company the villagers found the whole task mere play. There was a lot of merrymaking among women, and some gossip, too.

Lubele, high on his tree, leaned against the main trunk, his legs stuck between two branches. For a moment he had stopped working. He counted those present and those not. All were there: Kamuyuga, his two sons; Zaleme and Mashaka, Mbembela, Mulenge, Muyeya and Ngadindi. He was about to take it that all were there when Andunje came to his mind. Andunje was not there. Maybe there is some important reason for his not coming, Lubele thought.

The work went on until noon. Then the whole party walked in a line towards the home of Lubele. Dogs, a team of them, dashed to and fro past their masters. Sweat dripped down every face. Everybody was thirsty for the beer and there was a kind of force field that seemed to accelerate their motion. It pulled so strongly that their legs worked so fast, they were almost running. It was some distance from the compound of Lubele where the beer pots were installed. One would definitely not be able to smell it. Yet everybody sensed that he could.

The villagers at last got seated. Some on stools, some on mats and others on the ground. Former member of the King's African Rifles, Ngadindi, was installed to serve. That was a special office, as everybody knew. It meant quite a lot, to be awed and esteemed. It was a licence to avenge oneself, too. One could always ignore those who fell in his displeasure.

After drinking two, three bowls which were passed round, the neighbours took leave of Lubele, one by one. They went home to take their meals, wash and then in better dress come back to enjoy themselves in more relaxed moods.

The compound became deserted. Nganda was busy in the kitchen preparing lunch. Lubele, without changing the ragged khaki shorts he had put on at work, sat in the shade of the mango tree in the compound. He pulled the haft of his new hoe and began smoothing it with a bevel.

"Bulembe has grown fast over the two past years," Nganda broke the stillness of silence that had hung heavily in the air since the departure of Ngadindi, who left last.

"Indians especially. They have increased the population very greatly," Lubele agreed.

"And as I have heard nowadays it doesn't take much time to sell things. They say when you arrive at the market, hawkers snatch away all that you have."

"You don't even have to go that far. Hawkers stay at the riverside at *darajani*, along the path that comes to Mpunguta. Early at dawn they are already there waiting to compete for bananas and vegetables. This one tells you 'Bring bananas here. For all of them

I will give two shillings!' Another may say 'two and a half,' another can even say 'three'. You become puzzled and yield to anybody who pulls."

"Do you think that's a lie? That's not a lie. Yesterday it happened to Mugindi. They all jumped at her and tried to snatch away what she carried. They would have done it if it was not for her husband, Kamuyuga, who shouted at them."

"Did they give them?"

"No. The bananas and vegetables were already bought by some Indian." Here Nganda lowered her voice as if there were a person in the vicinity to overhear.

"Who was this Indian?"

"A new Indian. But she told me that I should keep this a secret."

"Who?"

"Mugindi."

"What secret?" Lubele raised his head, and stopped the bevelling.

"The name of the Indian, I don't remember it very well. It is_Charan, I think. He doesn't eat meat. Only vegetables. And Mugindi told me that he even buys *tajuni.*"

"What is his problem not to eat meat? Is he very old?"

"She says that he is not very old. Just like Kamuyuga or you."

"Then doesn't he have teeth?"

"Not him alone. I hear that his wife and children do not eat meat as well. So it can't be because of teeth. They have just come from India."

"Then what did you say was secret?"

"I as told not to say this. Maybe it is because they don't want other people to sell their things there."

When the meal was ready, Nganda came out of the kitchen bending low with a tray on which was porridge in a small aluminium dish. Besides the aluminium dish there was another small, multi-coloured dish. It contained neatly packed mushroom chips, and a little bigger bowl of water. She put down the big tray that contained these things before Lubele.

The dogs had already assembled. They looked at every action Lubele made. He immersed his right hand in the basin of water, then cut himself a big lump of porridge and dipped it in the mushroom dish. They traced the path the lump took until it disappeared into the mouth. But they seemed able to trace it even beyond. Hunger was distinctly expressed in their eyes.

"*Wee! Toka!*" he yelled at them.

The dogs retreated a bit. Lubele cut out a bigger lump, and tossed it at one of the dogs. The lump did not take much time in the air before it descended down the dog's throat. Lubele cut another lump and this time it was the turn of the other dog. There was no difference in the expression of hunger on their faces. Lubele then would take in one lump, the second and third being tossed at Kalibukufa and Fukara alternately.

When he finished eating, the two thin dogs still kept looking at him, then only a little differently from the beginning, but no satisfaction. Nganda came out again and fetched the utensils.

"*Toka, toka!*" Lubele shouted and turning round for a stone, he threw it at one of the dogs as they tried to flee. "Bwee, bwee!" Kalibukufa sounded as the stone hit him.

"Tomorrow I will go to town. Make sure that you pack bananas and vegetables in the big basket," Lubele instructed his wife.

"Which vegetables? If radishes, it is not possible. They are not ready for picking. There is no other type of vegetable."

"What then shall I take with me tomorrow?"

"Take bananas. Only bananas. That big basket, if full, will give not less than two shillings."

"Bananas are very heavy. Hii! You want me to go bald like the wife of Mulenge?"

"Hmm. Did she grow bald because of carrying things?"

"Yes. You want to argue?" Lubele said laughing. Nganda smiled.

"Then carry the *tajuni*. And since tomorrow Kamuyuga is going to town, too, then go with him. You may be able to sell *tajuni* to his Indian, Charan."

Twenty minutes later Kamuyuga pulled up. Nganda brought out a stool and put it beside Lubele. Kamuyuga did not sit but passed on to the kitchen. He stood at the kitchen door absent-mindedly. In his hand he rolled some crushed tobacco leaves in a piece of dry leaf of a maize cob. He lit the cigar and came out.

"We will sit here," Lubele, speaking from behind the house, told Kamuyuga. He had the two stools in his hands and proceeded to the shade behind the house. Kamuyuga came slowly, drawing on his cigar without interval until only a small piece remained.

He extinguished it and stuck it behind his earlobe.

"I hear that you are going to town tomorrow," Lubele said in tentative inquirement.

"I hope so. If I sleep well, I will start off very early in the morning."

At this moment Ngadindi made his appearance. He had changed the ragged working clothes and was then in a new khaki pair of shorts and a brown sweater which he had smuggled out of the K.A.R. He walked leisurely to where Lubele and Kamuyuga sat and seated himself on the ground. After greeting them he reached for the bowl of beer that lay near Lubele. The contents had divided into a thick opaque bottom and a clear top. He rotated the bowl carefully, stirring and mixing the contents. He brought the bowl to his mouth. The top part shone like a mirror and in it his moustache, twisted into two tufts, one on each end, almost touching the liquid, was reflected.

More and more people came. Women disappeared behind the wall into the backyard and men joined their already-warmed up colleagues behind the house.

The attention of the people was arrested when the *Jumbe* Mihanyo, made his appearance. He was a tall person, obviously clever and cunning. And when he appeared, everybody dried up. There was already that feeling of guilt in everybody present. A self-suspicion of having done something wrong spread like an epidemic. He was followed by two people, one of them being a headman. The other was Kadufi.

Lubele had noticed them even before they had reached his home. He went to meet them. They entered quietly. Kamuyuga followed Lubele and they stayed in the house drinking and talking with the honourable guests. With the Jumbe away from them, the people behind the house were enjoying some of their best hours in life.

The sun went down and a lot of noise had grown all over. In the backyard women sang, clapped and danced. The men outside were already up in staggering dances. Ngadindi kept firm at the beer pot.

Darkness befell the whole plain at length. There were no signs of rainfall that day. The air was filled with the pandemonium that hung heavily over the compound. Ngadindi brought some logs of wood and bark of *miombo* trees. He made a huge fire. The warmth seeped pleasantly deep into their bones, and their stomachs, which had till then been taking in cold beer, felt much relieved. Andunje had been there for more than half an hour. Ngadindi had noticed him arrive but did not care to give him anything. Andunje had not come to the *ushirika* that morning, and Ngadindi kept this in mind. Why did Andunje not come and explain it to him'! This vexed Ngadindi. Was Andunje so much proud? Ngadindi decided to show him the reaction he could put up.

Thus Andunje sat there, his lips and throat cracking with drought. He kept his eyes fixed at Ngadindi who, in his turn, always tried to evade them. Still, in the darkness, the two men could fel the tension that was building up between them.

Mashaka, son of Kamuyuga, had come there with his dog, Mapesa. The dog, which was a little distance away, barked at something. When the dog barked the noise came to a sudden stop and everybody turned to it.

"Mapesa, come!" Mashaka called the dog affectionately. The dog came wagging his tail humbly and lay in front of Mashaka beside the fire.

"Dogs are very good animals," Mbembela popped up. "I think they are second only to man among things." Then everyone became eager to argue and quite a number of voices erupted in unison. Then one fellow took over loudest and succeeded in putting off all the others.

"No. There is no animal superior to a monkey," he said "A monkey has everything that a man has except that it has more-- a tail. It has got palms, feet, arms, everything just like a man."

"No. If you had said that a cow is cleverer I would have agreed. Last year when I was working at Mikumi, my Indian sent me to look for a cow. I came to Bulembe to look for one. When the butcher at Mikumi failed to slaughter it, the next day the cow was seen back in Bulembe. It had come alone the whole distance!" Zayumba said.

"No, a chameleon is superior," put up another voice. "When it is in certain surroundings it takes the colour of that place and gives itself good camouflage. Have you ever imagined such super power?"

Andunje, who had up to then kept quiet, covered by a deep mysterious air, now got stirred by the conversation.

"No, that cannot be," he said. "In my opinion a mosquito is superior. It never bites on the blanket. It may keep groping about in the dark until it gets the feel of human flesh. Only then it can bite." Before Andunje could finish saying this, a great laugh broke up among the crowd and was sent clattering to the sky. Ngadindi, who was then just next to Andunje, laughed very loudly and provocatively in the face of Andunje.

Andunje trembled with anger. For a moment he knew nothing he could do. Anger accumulated in his chest like a wild storm that was waiting to be sparked off. The laughter did not end soon. People now laughed not only at what Andunje had said but also at what others had previously spoken.

Before people had noticed his anger, Andunje lifted one of the beer-filled vessels off the ground and sent it into the face of Ngadindi. The beer splashed on the face of Ngadindi and soaked into his brown K.A.R. sweater, the edge of the vessel banging hard on his nose. Andunje reached for a firestick that was burning red and flung it with full strength and hit Ngadindi in the stomach. Then he stood up and rushed into the backyard where the women sat. He reached his wife and gave himself some favourable camouflage under one of her *khangas*.

Not a moment elapsed before the long khaki shorts sounded, as they kept hitting against the thighs of the former K.A.R. member while he ran into the backyard after Andunje. He gave a hurried look all over. There was no sign of a man in the yard.

Everybody had stirred up. Mbembela and Zayumba came behind Ngadindi.

"Please, Ngadindi, ignore him," Zayumba begged of him.

"No, I want to show him."

"Please don't. You may kill him, Ngadindi."

Mbembela grabbed one of the bony, thin arms of Ngadindi and Zayumba the other. They led him back to the party, and Ngadindi walked back without resistance, in a manner much changed, like a cock after having done with a hen. The three resumed their places and nobody spoke of what had just happened.

In the backyard, Andunje slowly rid himself of his wife's *khanga*. He sat there for a quarter of an hour pondering over what had just happened, detail by detail, how he had flung the beer-bowl into the face of Ngadindi. He felt guilty and a kind of fear hung over him. Then his mind began to trace the whole cause of the affair. Slowly came the feelings of anger and hatred when he remembered how he had been sitting there without drinking. He had tried his best to bear the humiliation. It was painful, he concluded. He had to fight back. He felt the *khanga* still lingering in his arms. Shame oppressed him and he jerked himself up with such strength that he staggered forward almost falling over. He managed to stand upright again and with a somewhat firmer step moved out of the yard. When he came into sight of the drinking men he stopped to listen. He had expected to hear them speak about him. But he discovered that they talked about nothing in particular.

The figure of his enemy came to his notice first. It kept bending down now and again filling and refilling the beer vessels. Andunje now felt that Ngadindi must have grown bigger than before. His figure looked like that of a lion. He wanted to leap upon him and crash him to pieces, but he began feeling the vigour and courage, which had belonged to him when under the *khanga* of his wife, waning. He felt tiny. The cold of the night was getting the better of his bones and he spontaneously moved to where he had sat before, trying his best to avoid the notice of Ngadindi.

Zayumba had seen him.

"Don't start it again, Andunje," he warned him.

"Why?" Ngadindi broke up, his heart thumping loudly.

"Just let him. I will show him. If he thinks that staying at Pwani or going to *manamba* is to be clever, I will show him at I have not only been to Pwani, but have lived under the salt water.

By midnight all the beer was finished. Jumbe Mihanyo, accompanied by the headman and Kadufi, had left. Other people, one by one, collected their families and staggered their way home. The compound became quiet again. Drunken singing could be heard fading towards different directions from the compound of Lubele.

Zayumba, followed by Ngadindi and Mbembela, entered the house where they joined Lubele and Kamuyuga. There had been a fire in the house and the intruders sat around it.

"Baba, now I am leaving," Zayumba said, taking leave of his father-in-law.

"Thanks a lot. My greetings to your father, Chochocho."

"Ngadindi," Zayumba called him and pulled him by the arm.

Together they staggered past the narrow door and went out.

"I am going to sleep at your house, Ngadindi. Do you think I can go to Mkomolo and arrive there this day?" Zayumba said, imitating the voice of one of his Indian masters.

Ngadindi laughed. "This is up to you. Why do you drink so much when you know that you live behind the hills at Mkomolo? All this is due to your greediness for beer," Ngadindi teased his friend as they went.

A minute later, Kamuyuga left, leaving Lubele and Mbembela.

"I am not going home today. I will sleep here," Mbembela said, stretching himself on the floor. Lubele, who had started to doze, opened his eyes.

"But I don't have enough beds. I have tried to make one but the problem now is fibre. The *miombos* don't yield good rope this season. Now I don't know what to do with the bed."

"Rope?" Mbembela put up. "Why rope? Use skin. I have one bed woven with strips of skin. It has lasted I can't remember how many years."

"But if skin, then it should be cow's skin."

"Not necessarily. Even goatskin can do. But I can still bring you cow's skin."

"Do you have one? Then I will be most grateful."

"Ah, yes. I have more than one. I will bring you one. Don't worry." Mbembela could not even finish these words- before he fell asleep and snored, making the whole house echo like a cave of hungry cubs.

SEVEN

The cock-crow had become a monotonous song, but many people still kept in their beds. The large feet of Lubele wiped the cold morning dew from the moistened leaves and grass that lay deep on the narrow path to Bulembe. His left hand was stretched high, holding in position a big basket on his head as his right-gripped tight and raised his *kanzu* to the knees to prevent it from getting wet. In front of him walked Kamuyuga carrying in his right hand a basket of peas and radishes.

They walked in silence for long intervals. The huge basket huge filled with bananas and some *tajuni* pressed upon the head of Lubele with such weight that two huge veins on each side of his neck swelled out like pipes that were about to burst.

The sun was then rising from behind the Mbazala hills. The path was sloping towards the river that bounded the township.

Lubele and Kamuyuga could see a handful of people creeping near the edge of the bridge with eyes fixed upon them as they descended. Each of them had a basket or something with him. There were adults and some boys too. They looked much excited at the sight of the approaching peasants.

"When they shout at you, don't look at them or you will drop down your load and fall into the river. Walk stiffly. They want to buy things very cheaply these town Swahilis are very clever," Kamuyuga hinted to his neighbour. They soon came face to face with the group as they were about to cross the river.

"What are you carrying?"

"If bananas, come here."

"All radishes here!" The hawkers kept shouting at them.

Kamuyuga tore through the semicircle of hawkers quickly and Lubele, coming behind him floppingly and with the weight of his load now greater than ever, made a swoop leaving a cloud of flies buzzing over the hawkers. The hawkers hooted and laughed heartily.

"*Washamba hao, haoo . . .*" they jeered.

Lubele and Kamuyuga walked without looking back. Soon they were walking past Majengo. The houses built of mud and roofs were of grass thatch. There were no proper streets, only clusters here and there. There were small retail shops and on their walls paper advertisements were stuck: Pepsicola, Aspro, Melabon. Trays of *maandazi* supported on oil kerosene *debes* were common in front of houses.

They passed Majengo and were in sight of the market place. There were already some people there. The two kinsmen crossed the market square and reached the other ends. At the edge of the market ground two people were busy unpacking bundles of secondhand clothes and hanging them on a bamboo bar. There were numerous types of clothes- coats, trousers, *kanzus*. They crossed over to a house facing the market square. Kamuyuga halted at its front door. The doors of the house were still closed. Kamuyuga helped his neighbour put down the heavy load. Lubele sighed deeply. He felt his neck greatly compressed by the heavy load and he tried to stretch it painfully. The hair on his head lay flat. Flies swarmed noisily all about him.

They waited. People continued to flow into the market. Then the attention of the two men was caught by a man passing in front of them. He was wearing a white pair of shorts, a pair of white stockings, black shoes, a white shirt and a black tie. His face wore an air of permanent arrogance. His eyes were cast straightforward and he walked with a firm step, swinging his right hand like a soldier in parade while his left clasped files tightly to his side. Is clearly parted hair could be seen from where Lubele and Kamuyuga had stood.

"Do you see that man?" Kamuyuga asked his friend in a little more than a whisper.

"Yes. I see him."

"And do you know who he is?"

Lubele looked at the fellow more keenly for some few moments as the man disappeared behind a building. He shook his head.

"No, I don't know him. But I have seen him before at *bomani*."

"So this is Mr. Samuel. He is, they say, chief clerk in the *boma*. When you go there for some reason you will see there a bench outside the *boma*. You sit there until the messengers ask you what you want. You tell one of the messengers and he takes you into the *boma* to this man. Then he can tell you to come nearer. He asks you many questions as he writes. He goes on asking like that for a long time…"

"What does he ask?" Lubele questioned.

"Many things. If you have paid your tax, what is your age, if you have children, many things. Sometimes he can tell you to go and see the D.C."

Half an hour later the door of the house swung open. A short, thin Indian stood in the doorway. He was in his pyjamas and leather slippers. His mouth moved up and down chewing *tamboos*.

"Wait there," Kamuyuga told Lubele as he noticed that Lubele was about to hoist his basket and enter. The Indian did not say anything. He did not in fact seem to notice them. Kamuyuga stood there stupefied. This was none other than Charan himself. He went over to where the Indian had stood.

"Wait outside, just wait out there," Charan mumbled at Kamuyuga. Kamuyuga turned round rapidly, trying to make it seem casual and tightening his cheek muscles to force a smile.

"What is it?" Lubele asked eagerly.

"Nothing. It is him. Charan, my friend. He has come from, India very recently," Kamuyuga said, his eyes fixed at the door, expecting to be called in. They stayed there for a long while, their necks bending towards the door.

Half an hour elapsed. The market was already filled with people selling, buying, chatting. Others walked into shops purchasing their few daily needs. The sun was then high up in the sky, pouring its heat upon Lubele and his colleague, who still stood without much talking in front of the shop of Charan. They stayed thus for a long while. At last Kamuyuga mounted the steps and walked into the shop.

An Indian woman whom Kamuyuga knew to be Charan's wife was seated behind the counter. She sat in a big armchair wearing a pink silk sari. Kamuyuga stood opposite her and kept looking at her hard. Now and again a customer walked into the shop, asked for one thing or another. Mrs Charan would absently shake her head very lightly and without looking at the questioner. It appeared that the customers were familiar with the gesture. They seemed to understand her better that way for they didn't seem to wish to ask anything more or argue. The gesture bore more than words could hold. They would walk out silently looking down.

It came to Kamuyuga that he would not be able to win the attention of Mrs Charan by just standing like that. "Mama," he began, "I want to see Mr Charan." Mrs Charan looked at Kamuyuga for the first time. She knitted her brow in a kind of surprise.

"Charan, Charan. I want to see Mr Charan," Kamuyuga repeated with a desperate effort. Mrs Charan never said anything for a moment. She resumed her air of total absentmindedness, her left palm holding her cheek. Then she slowly tilted her head to her right and peered through a curtain that flopped lightly in the doorway. Fixing her eyes at the carpet she spoke something in her language as if addressing the carpet.

Kamuyuga fell back in bewilderment. He did not see the person she had been addressing. In the same language a voice came-from behind the curtain. This was Charan himself. Thus Mr. and Mrs. Charan spoke to each other for a while.

"Alli," she called three times. A thin voice responded and a man of about thirty years appeared. He was very dirty, wearing a ragged pair of shorts. His hair was filthy, as if mud had been smeared into it. Mrs. Charan beckoned Kamuyuga to bring in what he had.

Kamuyuga had all this while been watching without understanding whether what Mrs Charan was then doing was relevant to his question or not. He turned round and went out. He lifted his basket and re-entered. As Lubele lifted his, Kamuyuga signalled him to wait. Lubele let down the heavy basket, feeling much depressed. He began wondering why he had not sold his bananas to the hawkers at the riverside or at the market as they did the other days. As he directed his eyes to the market he noticed Mayeya and his wife. They were walking away, probably after selling their things. Lubele felt foolish.

Alli took the basket over from Kamuyuga, turned the radishes and the peas over and over before Mrs Charan. This time the landlady bent a little to have a look at the vegetables. Alli went on turning over the vegetables.

"No banana today?" she asked as he pulled out the drawer and gave Kamuyuga a shilling coin. Kamuyuga snatched the coin hurriedly. He turned round and signalled Lubele to bring in his bananas.

"There are bananas, too, Mama," he replied. Lubele, this time without much eagerness, hauled the bamboo-plaited basket and staggered in.

The basket was brought down before Alli, who took it to the feet of Mrs Charan. She accepted bananas only. She said she had already got radishes and peas; hence the *tajuni* remained in a heap in the basket of Lubele, without value. Pulling the drawer out a second time she picked another shilling corn and tossed it on the counter.

Kamuyuga kept gazing at Mrs Charan who, in her turn, kept holding her cheek and looking forward in the characteristic blank look that belonged to her. Kamuyuga, without saying anything more turned round to join his friend Lubele, who was already outside.

"Wee!" Mrs Charan yelled. Kamuyuga turned. "When will you come again?"

Kamuyuga, without taking much time to think, answered urgently. "Any day, Mama."

"How, any day? Tomorrow. Bring more radishes, do you hear?"

Kamuyuga wanted to disagree. He wanted to shout a "no". He felt unable. He only nodded in agreement.

Lubele had not stayed to wait for his friend. He went straight to where the second-hand clothes were sold and stopped there. Kamuyuga joined him.

"Which one do you want?" Lubele was asked by one of the fellows. He did not answer. He turned round to Kamuyuga, appealing for his advice.

"And how much money do you have?" Kamuyuga asked him. Lubele bent over his side as his right hand slipped down his chest. He brought out a tiny bundle wrapped up with bits of *kaniki*. He untied the bits one by one and heaped them at his feet. At last shilling coins reposed before his eyes. He dropped onto the purse the coin he had just received from Mrs. Charan. It fell with a relieving sound to his ears. He picked five of them, wrapped the purse with the bits of cloth one by one and slipped it down his chest.

"Nine shillings," he told the fellow.

"Which one do you want?"

The eyes of Lubele ran along the bamboo bar for a while and at last got stuck over a grey cloak.

"This one is twelve," the fellow said.

"I want one for nine."

Then the fellow knelt down and produced from a bundle, children's clothes, women's brassieres, and dirty underpants. Lubele shook his head and turned round to go when the fellow called him back.

"I will give you the cloak for nine and a half!" the fellow yelled. Lubele hesitate. "O.K., for nine!"

Lubele came back and got the cloak. He sprawled it out and examined it more closely. It was a thick, wooly, grey cloak with big, red letters on the back NANCY, it was written. He smiled and gave the money.

They stopped at the market many times to greet people they knew. From there they roamed about looking for little things in the shops for a long while.

It was about noon when, like two deserted ants, Lubele and Kamuyuga started for home. The sun had by then grown very hot and they began feeling tired and hungry. At Majengo they turned to the right to a house where four years before a niece of Kamuyuga was married. It was a small mud house. They were led into a room in the hack house. A grass mat was brought and sprawled on the earth floor. Lubele put aside his basket and slowly seated himself. Kamuyuga sat, too. A woman, the niece, came and sat at the door. She greeted them in Anyalungu. A little boy came running from the kitchen and clung to the neck of the woman.

"Is this that friend of mine?" Kamuyuga asked.

"Yes, it is he" the niece replied, smiling proudly and clasping the boy to her side.

- "And what is his name?"

"Athumani. Athumani, go and greet them. Greet your grandfathers," she told the boy, pushing him to the guests. Lubele stretched his hands to receive the boy but the boy declined and only kept staring at him. Lubele grabbed him. The boy struggled to free himself. Lubele released him as his fingers went numb at seeing the boy wriggle like that. Athumani ran after his mother into the kitchen.

Lubele and Kamuyuga were left sitting there alone, talking to each other. Lubele pulled the basket to his side and brought out the cloak.

"If you had chosen one with sleeves it would have been better. But it does not matter, though. When it is cold just put it on and have no worry," Kamuyuga remarked. Lubele did not appear to agree with the remarks of his neighbour. He kept gazing at the big red capitals, NANCY, for a long while. He could not read but he tried hard to reckon what it stood for. Kamuyuga, knowing what Lubele had been thinking of, snatched the cloak and looked hard at the letters.

"This was written there in Europe when it was being made. Not here," he said.

"Ah, this can't have been written here. It should be there in *Ulaya*," the other emphasized.

There was a sudden thundering of foot-steps in the backyard. A man in the uniform of a messenger pounded into, the kitchen. A minute later he came over to where Lubele and his colleague sat. -

"*Shikamooni, Wazee,*" he greeted them, standing with arms akimbo, the edges of his cap bathing in the sweat that flowed down his forehead. Even before the old fellows had

responded to the greeting, the messenger of the D.C. had vanished, thrusting his person into the little kitchen.

"Is this not the nephew?" Lubele wondered.

"It is him, *Baba* Athumani," Kamuyuga replied.

The young woman appeared again carrying a tray of food.

It was *ugali* with *kauzu.*

"Tell Athumani to come and eat with us," Kamuyuga told his niece as she went back. A moment after, Athumani appeared peeping from the door.

"Come," Lubele called him. The little boy smiled, and disappeared into the kitchen again.

"These are children brought up in the European manner."

"They want to sit at a table like the D.C.?" Lubele suggested.

"And all this is because of his father. He sees these things in the house of the D.C. and he acts same when he comes home. Have you seen the tobacco pipe the D.C. smokes?"

"Ah, yes. Almost all the times I have seen him he had the pipe with him."

"So *Baba* Athumani also has one like that. And you haven't heard him mimic the D.C. He talks exactly in the same voice the D.C. talks, and copies the walk very smartly. You would laugh very much," Kamuyuga related as he crushed the *kauzu* between his teeth.

"And can the child speak Anyalungu?"

"Aaah! I say these are children of another era."

The huge feet of *Baba* Athumani pounded the earth outside the kitchen and the messenger of the D.C. dashed out of the compound after taking a hasty meal in the tiny kitchen.

Up in the sky, Lubele could see black clouds gathering.

"It will rain today," he warned his companion. They finished eating and stood to go. Standing at the kitchen door, Lubele offered the *tajuni* which had till then remained in his basket. The niece came out and thanked them for their coming.

That afternoon the two little dogs, Fukara and Kalibukufa, bent their necks over the dug-out footpath that climbed to the Mpunguta hills, as if under the weight of their bone hearts. Their wet noses occasionally touched their master, Lubele, who walked in front of them. They trailed obediently, wagging their tails. There was something on the faces of the dogs, a kind of deep respect and admiration for Lubele. They seemed to see the incarnation of wisdom, among many other qualities, in him.

Lubele clinched firmly a club in his right hand as it rested at his shoulder. His knife was at his waist as usual, inseparable from him. It was not long since the hunting had begun and on that account there had not been any success yet, as far as Lubele knew. The sun, then quite low, still poured enough warmth. A brief bit of rain that had just fallen after the heavy noon rain had left the surface of the bare rocks still wet. Lubele was bored. On this particular day he had no mood for hunting. If it were not for the *tajuni* he had eaten for three days consecutively, he would not have attempted the foil.

A small bundle of firesticks lay just beside the footpath. Then the thoughts of Lubele suddenly vanished and gave way to move about the firesticks. There seemed to be no resting upon the head of the club, which he placed erect on the ground. His thoughts wandered.

He lifted the club at length and resumed the hunt. Not far off, the eyes of Lubele caught sight of a colony of mushrooms. He bent his stiff backbone and picked them, tied them in a bunch with some bark rope and carried them hanging by the rope in his fingers.

A cough came from amongst some bushes and pricked the attention of Lubele. It came quite distinctly, a voice somewhat familiar. He took some steps towards the bushes. The springing green bushes and grass were swept to and fro. Lubele neared. There was a woman stretched on the grass that now made a soft bed under the pressure of her struggling body. She struggled hard, her arms stretched out on her either side. Lubele bent over her.

"What is it, Ntandu?" there was no answer. "Ntandu, Ntandu...." He kept whispering.

Ntandu now lifted her legs and brandished them in the air wildly. The black *kaniki* cloth which was tied above her breasts dropped from her knees and she became almost naked. She went on writing like that for some time. At last she stopped, laying her legs stretched before Lubele.

"Stomach, stomach. It is aching," she muttered.

Lubele left her with a leap. The dogs, too, leaped to follow him. After not more than two minutes, he came back with some young, fleshy twigs.

"Chew on this," he said, putting them in the mouth of Ntandu. His eyes kept looking at the small mouth of Ntandu as it moved slowly up and down, chewing and sucking the juice out of the twig.

It was a look filled with pity at first but it soon changed into a long, fond look. This was Ntandu, that widow he had ignored all the time. He had never bothered to discover what she actually was. But now it all lay before him.

Ntandu still lay there motionless, the fit seeming to subside. Her exposed thighs glimmered in the last rays of the reddening sun in the west. Lubele, still bending over her, felt a whimsical desire. Involuntarily, he let his hand pass between the soft thighs smoothly.

She gave deep sighs. It appeared that she had recovered somewhat. The scene then transformed dramatically. It seemed that the fit which had attacked Ntandu now extended to Lubele. But this one was of a different nature. He kept fondling her.

"No, no," she protested, opening her eyes and pushing the cloth down her knees with much strength. "No, Lubele, no." For a brief moment, Lubele was disappointed. Then he changed to exasperation. Ntandu saw it in his eyes and she worried.

"No, Lubele. I mean not today," she pleaded. Lubele came to himself and for the first time he swung his neck round and noticed the presence of the dogs sitting opposite him. They had been watching very attentively as if there was a report they had to draw up.

"*Tokeni!*" Lubele sent clattering at them. They immediately dashed away, humbly wagging their tails. Ntandu came to her feet and went over to her bundle of firewood.

The sun was then setting, and for Lubele the resumption of hunting became a time-wasting endeavour. He picked up his hunting tools and mushrooms and shuffled his feet home.

EIGHT

Three days later Mugindi, Kamuyuga's wife, brewed some beer. This was for no ceremonial purpose but simply a means to get cash. Lubele had gone to Bulembe to sell his bananas early in the morning. He came back to Nlimanja quite late in the afternoon.

He sat outside the kitchen taking his supper that evening, when he heard the singing that was propelled by the wind from Mpunguta.

"How is the beer at Mpunguta today? I didn't pass by the house of Kamuyuga. And in the town I met Kamuyuga himself but I forgot to ask him. Do they say it is good?"

Nganda drew smoke from her tobacco pipe many times before she answered.

"I haven't been there today. I thought I would go there now."

"You want to go where?" Lubele said with emphasis.

"Where, how?" Her husband's question had come coldly into the ears of Nganda. She sensed a quarrel.

"If you wish to drink beer, I will tell Mugindi to send you some. But you shouldn't go there. If we give you such privileges you take them for times to show off yourselves before men. This I don't like. I have always been telling you but you seem not to hear." Lubele recalled a time two days before at a beer party when he saw Nganda dancing with Ngadindi. He had wanted to assault one of them but he was drunk. The incident had nonetheless remained in

his heart and he knew that one day it would erupt.

Lubele finished eating and went into the house. He re-appeared after a little while wearing his cloak and smoking a cigar.

"I am going to Mpunguta now. You will have to stay here." Nganda did not answer.

The bare feet of Lubele kept pounding the earth along the faintly-seen path that sloped down to the river Mfele. He drew on the cigar hard and continuously, with a trail of smoke following him. Involuntarily Lubele's head swung round and his eyes spied something following him.

"*Wee!* Kalibukufa, *toka!*" he shouted. The dog darted back home.

For a time the thoughts of Lubele were centred on nothing in particular. He listened to the sounds that came from the bush.

He wondered how many times he had just ignored those tiny entities. The insects, too, were something. They existed. He cursed the idea that he, too, could have been created one of those. He wondered if he would tolerate sitting in the bush like that while listening patiently to the merrymaking that came from Mpunguta.

He puffed more on the cigar. But the crickets came to his mind again. Would he really enjoy it if he had been created a cricket? Surely he wouldn't, he confessed to himself. A feeling of deep thankfulness accumulated to him. He realized that he owed much to whoever created him a human being, and a man in particular. The way he managed his home affairs, for instance. He recalled the little quarrel he had just had with Nganda. The way he had ended it. As supreme of the household he might have ended the matter much differently. He could, for instance, take his skin whip Mid thrash Nganda. Nobody would ask him. Even *Jumbe* Mihayo himself wouldn't dare.

By then he had reached the river Mfele. He hardly noticed it and went on with his thinking. The cigar was now reduced to only a short stub that made his lips feel hot. He tossed it away as he started climbing his way up the hill to Mpunguta. At that elevation he was not able to hear much of the merrymaking.

He took up his thoughts again without having suffered much interruption. He felt that there was a virtue within him. It was something of leadership or a kind of administrative ability. This brought to his reasoning the case of Nganda with Ngadindi again, the way he had just let the affair vanish like smoke.

Then, like rays of the sun falling upon the landscape as it emerges out of a hindering cloud, his thoughts suddenly fell upon her. He had been thinking of her for the last three days. Ntandu. And since this widow came to his mind, the large feet of Lubele were left totally to see the way on their own. They had to grow eyes, besides other senses, to carry him to Mpunguta. Ntandu. He recalled her small figure, and it kept twinkling before his eyes. He recalled everything, the bushes that hid her that day, the reddening sun that was about to set in the western horizon, the thighs that glimmered in the last rays of sunlight, the dogs, the mushrooms and all. The words she had spoken had left a clear ringing in his ears. He thought he could hear her say, "No, Lubele, not today." Probably he would meet her there, he predicted, and therefore things would fill to the brim.

At Mpunguta people sat in many small clusters. A huge fire was lit beside the large pots that contained the beer. Mugindi was busy selling it and collecting the coins from some other women who assisted her. There were many women sitting close to the fire. They sat without drinking. They only talked. Those who had babies on their backs only listened to the weight of the live bulks. Men sat further away from the ring of women around the beer pots. There were Mbembela, Ngadindi, Zayumba, Mulenge, Andunje and the two sons of Kamuyuga. No people from afar.

Occasionally a man called a woman to where he sat and asked her to sip a bit. On many such occasions she would not retire until the bowl emptied. She would, even then, stay there singing to her benefactor and wait for him to give out some other ten cent-coin and get the bowl refilled.

When Lubele came to the scene, the place was calm. The merriment he had heard from Nlimanja had died down. Only the women shouted. Lubele said a greeting, and the noise died away. Everyone responded in his own way and it came up in a single murmur. Zayumba came near to his father-in-law, a bowl in his hands. He greeted him and gave him the bowl to take some few gulps. Lubele drank a bit

and replaced the bowl in the hands of Zayumba. After Zayumba followed Ngadindi, and some few others. Some brought their beer vessels with them and others only came to shake hands. At last came Mugindi with some little beer in a bowl for Lubele to taste. Lubele took out a ten-cent coin and offered it to her. She brought back to him a bowl filled to the brim.

For all this time the eyes of Lubele had wandered searchingly for Ntandu but he had not seen a single sign of her. He then took to scrutinizing the clusters more closely. He saw her at last. She was there. He wanted to call her to him and let her gulp down the contents of the bowl. He needed her to sit there, beside him, whatever the cost, if she drank all the fifty cents that he had under his cloak.

Ntandu did not look in his direction. Lubele tried to, endure. Should he call her? But no not then. She would come by herself, and if not then he would call her, but at a later time.

Half an hour elapsed and the place took on the charateristic liveliness of a beer party. People sang and danced and made all sorts of noise. Mbembela stood up, clapping and hopping with both legs together towards the clusters of women. The women stirred up. They clapped and sang for him. Mbembela kept the hopping dance going. Now there was a lot of noise in the compound and even the men sitting away from the women became amused by the dance. Lubele watched. Then Mbembela hopped to where Ntandu had sat. He stopped and bent upon her to look into her eyes. She sat still. Mbembela started the song again, this time singing into the ears of Ntandu and not hopping any more. The other women then stopped singing for him and he went on alone, bending at the side of Ntandu. He sang:

Ambe anganga majolo
Funyuunyu andi udende.
Udende ndi mdala chichi!

People of antiquity had proclaimed
Toothlessness is nothing faulty.
Faulty is a woman with a barren womb!

Ntandu jerked herself to her feet and went to sit at another place. Mbembela went on singing that song and followed Ntandu. Ntandu smiled shyly but just looked down. Mbembela came over to her again. He bent upon her as he had done before. Ntandu looked at him and smiled. Then suddenly she was vexed.

"Mbembela, why do you act like a child?" she reproached him.

"Aaah, you are a widow and not a barren woman, your husband died before he could give you a single child, eh? Isn't that what you say? But he was not the only one who could do it and it will be discovered if you are barren or what."

All the other women laughed and they urged him to sing and press on her. Ntandu felt as though she were being used as a toy and her annoyance heightened.

"I don't like this, Mbembela." she barked at him again.

"Shemeji," a voice came from Mugindi. *"Shemeji,* why not buy her *pombe?* She can't agree without buying her beer." All the other women laughed and sympathized with Mugindi. The merriment heightened.

"Is that true?" Mbembela enquired.

"Yes....." The women took it in unison. Mbembela took out ten cents and offered it to Mugindi. Mugindi filled a vessel with beer and gave it to Ntandu. Mbembela sat beside her and put his arms around her as she drank. Ntandu gulped a little and put the bowl down.

"Drink drink, drink. What do you fear?" Mbembela said, lifting the bowl back to her mouth. Ntandu hesitated at first but slowly raised it again and drank some more.

"Be happy when you see that Mbembela is around, be happy Because Mbembela can give you beer." He spoke this and then slowly, pulling her to his side, he whispered into her ears, "And he can give you children, too."

Lubele had been watching without missing a detail. His heart thumped and sweat oozed from his pores. His eyes enlarged greatly as if to pop out of their sockets. His hair stood on end and he quivered. Anger had overcome him. At first he had the thought that he should prevent Mbembela from following Ntandu when she ran away. But when he recalled to himself the people who were around, particularly his son-in-law, Zayumba, he refrained. And it then appeared that Mbembela had won her. Lubele continued thinking hard. He got a plan and it relieved him a bit: to humiliate Mbembela before the women there and disgrace him.

"Mbembela," he called.

Mbembela did not hear. Lubele called a second time, his voice shaky and coarse. There was a sudden break of silence. Mbembela, seeing that somebody had called him, wanted to respond but without a breach of his sovereignty. He asked, "Who calls me?"

"Here, you are called," Zayumba directed him. Mbembela regretfully loosened the warm arms of Ntandu, which by then were tied around him. A minute later he was standing before Lubele.

"Where is the skin?" Lubele asked, with great urgency in his voice.

"Skin? What skin?" Mbembela had foreseen the plot. "You forget, isn't it?" Lubele hardly spoke clearly. The words gushed out almost incoherently.

Other people listened and watched.

"I don't know anything of what you are talking about."

"Mbembela, what did you say that day at my house when you slept beside the hearth? You said that you would bring me a cowskin. That day there was beer at my house."

"Me, I am not aware of anything. I don't know anything about skins. Am I *Bwana Nyama?*"

Lubele's lips went numb with anger. He only stared. "O.K., Mbembela, but don't pass by my house."

"I will pass."

"Eeeeh?"

"Yes, I will, even today."

"You will see."

"Me? See what?" Saying this Mbembela retired and sat clinging to Ntandu as before.

Lubele, without adding anything more, stood up and left the place. Nobody could speak to him and be heard. The beer he had bought he left on the same spot where Mugindi had brought it. The silent crowd just gazed at him as he disappeared homewards.

Four hours elapsed. It was becoming more and more chilly as time passed. The moon was shining very brightly and showered its rays upon the ridges of Mpunguta and Nlimanja. All quiet except for the sounds of the thickets and the merrymaking that still came from Mpunguta. Two shadows staggered their way along the slope from Mpunguta. They sang heartily. It was a male and a female clinging to each other. They made several stops on their way down the hill to sing and dance. They sang and danced until some few metres from the house of Lubele. Then they stopped.

"Why do you stop, Ntandu?"

"No, no."

"Why? Let's go, How are you, woman? Now I come to know that your husband died because of such type of trouble. And he died without even leaving you pregnant. Are you a *uhichi*? I have given you a lot of beer. You have drunk all my forty cents. You don't know what it is to be loved, eh?" He pulled her.

"No, Mbembela. I don't mean that I don't want to come. Please let us avoid the house of Lubele. Let's pass in the bush."

"Ah, woman! What do you think Lubele is before me?" Mbembela said, staggering, and taking the arm of Ntandu he pulled her. Ntandu grumbled but at last yielded and was clinging to him again. They went on. When they reached the house of Lubele they stopped again.

"Why do you stop, Ntandu? You are an *uhichi*. This I know. In front of people you say you feel shy and now we are all alone here, still you want to resist me. I'm tired of you now. You are not a girl, are you?" Mbembela said, looking into her eyes.

"Ah, Mbembela you always speak nonsense."

"Nonsense how? I know all your dealings with men."

"Who, what men?"

"What! Now, you want to argue?" he asked, shaking her "Kamuyuga did it to you that day."

"Which?"

"That day there was beer at the house of Lubele. Kadufi and many others have told me."

Ntandu did not say anything.

"Do you still argue? That day, at the river Mfele, there in the cold." He laughed and started singing merrily again as they were passing the house of Lubele.

Ambe anganga majolo
Funyuunyu andi udende.
Udende ndi mdala uhichi!

Before he had finished singing this song a long strip of Hippo hide ran across his back. Lubele was already upon him. Before Mbembela came to realize what was really happening, Lubele had thrashed him all over his body. Mbembela yelled madly and the beer vanished from his veins. He staggered into the bush until he left the reach of the long thing. Still Lubele was behind him. They fought like two wild cats fighting for females. At length Lubele stopped.

Mbembela, crying all the while, took the path back to Mpunguta. He ran without looking back until he crossed the river Mfele. Then he stopped. His whole back ached acutely and drunkenness had shaken off his person.

"Lubele, you are very foolish. Uncivilized dog," Mbembela yelled, standing in the moonlight and looking at Lubele on the other hill.

"O.K. But now you have seen who is cleverer between us."

"You think yourself very great, *shenzi...*"

"Alright, but now I am sure you won't pass by my house. And the day I see you again you will enjoy the same thing."

"We will see!"

"O.K. You think that to have been to *manamba* is *ujanja*. Now I have shown you that you are not."

They exchanged curses and names like that until Lubele decided to retire. He reached the spot where he had leaped upon Mbembela but Ntandu was not there.

NINE

Two days had passed since the affair. Lubele had never gone out of his home. He did not receive any news about Mbembela.

It was in the afternoon. He was sitting in his compound basking in the sun when Kadufi came. Lubele fetched a stool from the kitchen and gave it to him. Kadufi seated himself without a word. After a brief exchange of greetings the two kept looking at each other like two wild cats. Kadufi had never been to the house of Lubele on a visit like that before, and Lubele suspected a special reason for this visit. Kadufi, too, felt uneasy. He did not waste much time before he told his mission.

"*Jumbe* calls you."

These words wrung the heart of Lubele and stirred up defiance in him.

"Jumbe?"

"Yes, Mihanyo."

"And what does he want to do with me?"

Kadufi did not add anything for the time. He kept gazing at the door of the tiny kitchen. The heart of Lubele beat faster and faster.

"When, did he say?"

"This evening." After saying this, Kadufi took his leave.

In the compound of Mihanyo that evening, Lubele found Kadufi sitting opposite the *jumbe,* their hands stretched out to receive the warmth of the fire that was burning between them. Lubele entered. There was no stool given to him. He sat away from the two and said a greeting. Mihanyo did not answer.

"Come near," Kadufi told Lubele. Lubele was alarmed by the position in which Kadufi appeared to install himself in this case. He suspected already that he was a kind of mouthpiece of the *jumbe.* But he did not recognize Kadufi for any position, high or low. He kept inert despite Kadufi's glaring at him inquisitively.

Kadufi could feel the pride of Lubele. He looked into the eyes of Mihanyo and read something in them, and with that, too, he read his duty.

"Lubele," he called, in a tone of address he knew would wound the other man. "I came to tell you that the *jumbe* calls you and you ask rudely, 'What for?' You know that the *jumbe* is under the chief, who is under the D.C. and you dare make yourself very big before them?"

Lubele did not say anything but slowly crept near to the fire. An urge to jump at Kadufi and do to him what he had done to Mbembela two days before filled Lubele. But then Mihanyo turned his head round for the first time. He cleared his throat and spoke.

"Do you know that you have done something very bad to Mbembela?" he asked. But before he had even finished saying this Kadufi took over.

"You are very proud, Lubele. You think that it is your right to demand other people's property?"

Lubele went wild. "Shut up, Kadufi. You are not *Jumbe*. If you think that you can talk to me like that you can ask Mbembela. I can show it to you, too."

"Listen, Lubele," Mihanyo interrupted. "You are an elder and not a *muhuni*. Mbembela came to me yesterday. He complained that you whipped him very badly. Now I want to tell you one thing, that this is very serious. You may even go to jail if Bwana D.C. bears this. I want to help you before this matter goes that far."

The wife of Mihanyo, who had been listening to all in her kitchen, spoke. "Yes, it is not good for such a good person to be jailed. Help him."

"Now go and bring ten shilling," Mihanyo sent the words coldly into the ears of Lubele.

"I don't have," Lubele said.

"Mmmh," the wife in the kitchen started. "He sells bananas every day. He has it," she said.

"Listen, Lubele. I am not to solicit something which has no meaning to me. I just do this for your sake. It is for your safety.

If you don't want then I will go and tell the D.C. to take you to jail. Now go and bring the ten shillings."

The *jumbe* was solemn. Lubele, too, saw it. He felt a light sweat break out on his forehead.

"Maybe on Monday. I will send my bananas to town and maybe I can find some," Lubele answered with consternation.

"Or to make things easier . . ." Here the jumbe lifted his eyes and eyed Kadufi. He seemed to hesitate. But he continued at length. "Bring this coat you are putting on," he said, pointing at the cloak Lubele had been wearing.

"Or send him to the D.C. if he denies. Ah!" the wife of Mihayo put in. " Are you to be soliciting like a child?"

Lubele took off the cloak. Mihayo received it offhandedly.

Ten minutes elapsed and there was no more talk of the affair. Mihanyo exchanged some few questions with his wife about the little things that had to do with their household. Then again, as if not conscious of his actions, the *jumbe* began to examine the woolly cloak which lingered in his arms. He noticed that it had no sleeves. No, he thought. That was not a cloth for him. Soon, he read the capital letters, NANCY, that came to his eyes. No. He didn't like it. It also gave out a smoky smell. No.

"Take this coat. You will bring me the ten shillings. Or if you can't then you will bring a cock. This you can't deny. Or if you want to refuse, then try."

Lubele had many arguments against this judgement in his heart but his tongue became paralysed. He kept his silence and the *jumbe* took this silence for submission.

"Kadufi, go with him and bring the cock," the *jumbe* ordered. Kadufi stood up and instantly Lubele did too. Mihanyo looked at Lubele, who was walking away. He said, "Now, Lubele, you can be at ease. Just bring the cock. I know how I can fix up these matters with Mbembela."

Kadufi walked about four metres behind Lubele. They walked silently and very uneasily. Ten minutes later they arrived at Nlimanja. Nganda was in her kitchen. Lubele stood before the kitchen door for a while, still feeling very disturbed in the presence of Kadufi. He called Nganda to him. They went into the house and after a minute or so they reappeared, Nganda carrying a cock in her arms. Kadufi neared her and grabbing the cock in his arms without a single word, he disappeared. Lubele looked at him for a long while before he had disappeared. Anger filled him and he wondered why he had not taken the leather thing and given him a good whipping instead of the cock.

Early next morning Lubele was at the house of Kamuyuga. They sat in the house basking in the fire.

"Since that day we have not been seeing each other," Kamuyuga, began looking at Lubele, smiling. "That day," he continued, "when you were very angry with Mbembela. We all thought that we could not make you cool down."

"You mean that day at the beer-party here?" Lubele poured in, laughing. "And did you hear what I did to the fool?"

"I just heard that you whipped him. Only that. Maybe you can tell me much more."

"The dog passed at my house as he had insisted. And I whipped him very finely." Lubele displayed the manner of the whipping by the swinging of his right hand. "He ran like a rat."

Kamuyuga laughed uproariously, leaning back against the wall.

"But that man, Mbembela," he added, "he is a good runner. I tell you he ran faster than a deer or otherwise I would have killed him. But even so I can't imagine how he is feeling now."

The narrative ended and they bent over the embers, which Kamuyuga kept poking with his big toe. There was a silence while each wandered far and near in his thoughts. Then Lubele spoke at last.

"Mbembela had gone to Mihanyo thinking that maybe I would go to jail. But I have done it off with the *jumbe*. He thought that he is cleverer."

"And what happened at the house of Mihanyo?"

"He wanted a cock and I gave it."

Mugindi came into the house and greeted Lubele. She stayed for a little while and then quit, leaving the men enveloped in silence.

"And what about you?" Lubele asked, looking at Kamuyuga in the face. "Were you at home all these two days?"

"No. Yesterday I went to town. Charan had gone to Daisalama. Did you know of that?"

"No, I didn't. Only once I happened to pass at his shop but I saw only the wife."

"So he had gone to Daisalama and it is only two days ago that he came back. I saw him yesterday for the first time since his arrival and I will go there tomorrow. I will take him some bananas, too."

"I will also wish to go to town tomorrow. I will carry bananas but I also wish to go and see Geregoli. I want to get news of Lunja. Do you know that I don't get any news of him?"

"How can you get any news? Does he know how to write letters?" Kamuyuga wondered.

"No, doesn't, but can't he ask those who know to write him even a bit of paper to send to us?"

"That is true."

It was about ten o'clock next day when the two kinsmen crossed the river that bounded Majengo and the township. They walked slowly and that day, they didn't carry very heavy loads. It wasn't like other days, a day for selling provisions. It was rather a day with speciality. The men talked voraciously as they went along.

"Was it yesterday when you told me of your case with Mbembela and that you have settled it?" Kamuyuga asked.

"Yes, yesterday when I came to your home in the morning."

"So it was yesterday in the evening then. Kadufi came to my house. He was very drunk."

"Yesterday, you say?" Lubele asked, closing up the distance between himself and Kamuyuga, who had been walking ahead.

"Yes, yesterday. I was in my house with my elder son, Zaleme, eating food. We called him to share the meal with us but he declined."

"Where did he drink? Was there beer anywhere yesterday?"

"Aaah, there was some little beer at Mpunguta. The wife of the old catechist teacher, Antoni, had made some. Do you know this Antoni? He comes from Ngaza Mission and it is about a year or so that he has been here."

"Aaah, Antoni? I know him," Lubele affirmed. "One day he came to my home at Nlimanja and asked me if I was baptized. I refused and since that day he doesn't pass at my house. And I hear that he also steals."

"Oohoo . . . him? Pray he doesn't pass at your house," Kamuyuga confirmed. He went on.

"One day I was away in the town and my wife had gone to the river to fetch water. The sons, too, were away. It was when Mugindi was coming back from the river. She heard the clucking of a hen. At first she thought that it was the dog of Muyeya, Joni, because that dog also goes for chickens. But when she came into the backyard she found Antoni running after the hen trying to catch it. And because he did not know that he was being watched he went on running after the hen while Mugindi watched him. The hen ran about and at last it entered the kitchen through a hole. He wanted to go in and catch it but he first turned round to see if people had been seeing him. Then he saw Mugindi."

"And what did Mugindi do all this while?"

"She had only been standing, watching, with the pot on her head. So when Antoni saw her he only smiled foolishly, standing where he was. Mugindi went into the kitchen to put down the pot and when she came out he was gone."

"Ah!" Lubele gasped. "If it had been me, I would have used my hippo whip on him. I tell you that he would never repeat." Kamuyuga grunted in assent.

But is he not employed and does he not get pay? I thought that these people working for the missionaries have a lot of money. How now?"

"Ah may be. But not this Antoni. His wife sells bananas and pombe to get money, like yesterday. She made some beer and sold to get money."

"They walked on.

"But these people," Kamuyuga started after leaving the theme for the time, "these missionaries are very powerful. It is only that there are no white men at the catechist school at Mpunguta that we donn't feel much of their existence."

"What do they do?" Lubele asked.

"Ehee... you have not run into their dominion. Try one day to argue with them. Even the D.C. is showing a lot of respect to them." Kamuyuga turned round to face Lubele. He could see that what he had been telling him did not sound true to Lubele. "Do you remember that year I made frequent visits to Mshenye?"

"And do you know Masharabu of Mshenye, that fellow who sells the best snuff at the market?"

"Oh . . . this one everybody knows."

"So Masharubu had not offered anything to the church for three years and he had not gone to pray for many months. Not that on Sundays Masharubu was never to be seen at the church; he went there but stayed outside selling his snuff to those who passed there going in and out of the church.

"So one day Mashurubu happened to run into one of the white priests. He was asked why he had not given the yearly offerings. Masharubu, you know argumentative he is."

"Oh! Masharubu? I hate him only for that."

"So when he was asked this, Masharubu appeared to argue and tease the priest. He was slapped in the face just like a child."

Lubele was agitated by the revelation. He felt some heavy thing press hard on his heart. He wished that this priest could be punished. The hatred he always had for Masharubu due to his argumentative nature suddenly vanished. He got the feeling that Masharubu was one of a large group in which he, too, was a member.

"Is this true?" he asked.

"You go and ask anybody living in Mshenye. He will tell you the same thing."

"And what did Masharubu say?"

"Masharubu's pomposity carried him quite far. He sent this case to *Bwana Shauri* – that other European shorter than the D.C. Do you know him?"

"Oh, *Bwana Shauri*? I know him quite well."

"So he told *Bwana Shauri* that the priest had slapped him. And when the priest appeared before *Bwana Shauri*, the case ended up in less than five minutes and Masharubu was warned not to think himself clever,"

"And what did *Bwana Shauri* do to the priest?" Lubele asked, eager to hear of justice done.

What would you expect him to say? When the priest entered, he was already hot with temper. He said, 'Do you listen to this dog? He doesn't give the offerings, and he doesn't attend mass either. Do you sympathize with him?' And immediately after saying this he left the office and got into his car. He told *Bwana Shauri* that he couldn't waste his time with that foolish case. And what I have narrated has only been passed on by the clerks in the office of *Bwana Shauri* who had overhead from their offices. It is not from Masharubu himself."

"Why? Does he hide?"

"No, he doesn't hide. The case and everything was done in English. Masharubu himself heard nothing except for the warning he was given. All the rest he hears from people just as I did."

The story had gone deep into Lubele. He never said anything but walked silently, stooping low over the path.

They had reached Majengo. Neither of them spoke. Then Lubele got the feeling that there was something they had neglected somewhere in their conversation. He thought hard for a while and two minutes later he caught the point.

"What did Kadufi say? You did not finish your tale," he reminded Kamuyuga.

"Oh, yes. I was about to forget it. What did I say last about him?"

"You reached the point that he declined to eat food at your house."

"Yes. Kadufi was very drunk and he told me that he had come to inform me that he was stepping down from the responsibility he has been handling over the village affairs. He said he no longer wanted to be a court elder."

"Elder of which court?" Lubele asked, shocked.

"That of the *Jumbe* Mihanyo."

"Then nobody will recognize Mihanyo as *jumbe. So is* that why Kadufi keeps following about Mihanyo wherever he goes?"

"I even came to realize this very lately."

"I don't mind. And even if he continues to be a court elder or what, I can whip him anytime I find him naughty," Lubele said firmly.

"And the reason for his stepping down is that you insulted him, and before the *jumbe* himself and his wife, and that Mihanyo let a court elder be humiliated."

"Did he say so?"

"Ah, this is only part of it. He went on to say that Mihanyo is not a good *jumbe*. He doesn't count court elders, that he took the cock you gave him while he, Kadufi, who was insulted, did not get anything." Kamuyuga halted again and they stood facing each other, this time on the market ground. They walked to a shade where Lubele put down the basket of bananas and sat. Kamuyuga continued narrating as he stood before his kinsman.

"Kadufi added that he was told by Mbembela that the *jumbe* will trifle the case because you have given him a bribe, and that he has advised him to send the case to the chief and if possible - and this will be possible he said —Mbembela should take a he-goat to the chief as bribe, too. He said that this year he will see who is cleverer between you and him."

Kamuyuga finished imparting his information and took leave of Lubele, who was to stay there selling his bananas, while Kamuyuga proceeded to the shop of Charan.

"If you finish selling before I come back then come and fetch me at the shop of Charan," Kamuyuga told Lubele as he walked away.

At four o'clock Lubele finished selling the bananas. All the while he had been sitting under the tree, Kamuyuga could be seen sitting outside the shop of Charan. Lubele, holding the basket in one hand, walked to where Kamuyuga sat.

"Have you been able to see him?"

"No, not yet. Charan is away, his wife says. But she has not told me where he has gone."

"I have finished selling the bananas and maybe now I should go and see Geregoli. If you see Charan before I come back, then wait for me here," Lubele instructed.

Lubele walked down the street slowly, trying hard to ignore and suppress the many wild ideas that popped up in his head. The weather had changed all of a sudden. A half hour before, the sun had been near to roasting the old bodies of the two peasants, making sweat stream down and their armpits smell. But then it had turned out to be very cloudy and the wind was blowing hard over the little town's streets, hurling bits of rubbish and blowing backwards the cloak Lubele wore. He wrinkled his face in an attempt to prevent his nostrils from sucking in dust. The sweat that had seemed endlessly flowing had then evaporated, leaving tiny white crystals all over him.

The thoughts of Lubele wandered far and near, ranging from the new thing Kadufl was cooking up for him to the remembrance of his son, Lunja. He thought he could picture the youth — a totally changed young man who would speak the Swahili language even more fluently than Kamuyuga could.

At last Lubele reached the house of Gregoli. There was no sign of him. All the doors were tight in their frames. Lubele stood there for not less than twenty minutes, waiting to catch anybody who chanced to come out, so that he could be able to make enquiries. But nobody did and the whole building looked dead. He turned to go back. When he arrived at the shop of Charan, Kamuyuga had gone in. Lubele remained outside waiting.

The clouds went on gathering and the wind went on blowing harder and harder. The same boredom which had been evident on the face of Kamuyuga as he had been sitting outside the shop of Charan could now be seen on that of Lubele. The market and the whole town in general had become deserted. It had all become very quiet except for the whipping of the wind. Not much later the town took on a new liveliness by the occurrence of an unexpected interruption.

A lorry rumbled down the road from Dar es Salaam and stopped at the shop of Khanji. It was an old Austin lorry with a wooden body that had two forms along its sides. Some passengers sat on the forms, others squeezed at the feet of those who sat on the forms, between the many heaps of luggage.

Lubele, who that day had longed to see Lunja, entertained the wishful thought that the passenger lorry had carried his son in it, too. This feeling was really strong and it carried him slowly towards the lorry. He didn't go very near but stood at the edge of the market square and leaned against a tree. Twenty people came out of the lorry, stretching themselves painfully as they came. Lunja, Lunja, Lubele spoke in his heart. But his son was not there. Lubele crept back to the shop of Charan across the deserted market square and resumed his position outside the shop on the cold cement steps.

Two of the men who had just alighted, accompanied by two women carrying babies on their backs, re-entered the lorry, and it started down the street. The others picked up their wooden suitcases and other luggage, and disappeared in the dirty town's alleys and streets.

TEN

Chief Gumwele sat on the verandah of his palace. He had put on a black suit that day. A black *mpingo* stick carved in the shape of a snake was held in his two hands, between his thighs, and occasionally he raised it and let it drop, tutting on the hard cement floor. Three elders in *shukas* slung over their shoulders sat at his sides. There was not much talk.

"These three days the passenger lorry has never come to Bulembe from Dar es Salaam. Maybe it is due to rain," Chief Gumwele, said looking in the direction of the town.

"It has arrived only a short while ago. It is that bigger one," an elder informed him.

"Has it arrived?" the chief wondered. "Maybe it was when I was sleeping inside."

"Yes, it is that time you were inside sleeping."

The rain would fall but not before two hours, for the wind blew very strongly, drifting the black clouds on and on. The compound of the chief wore its characteristic silence. A column of smoke rose above the tin chimney from the kitchen in the backyard. In this backyard, too, there were the two messengers, Magadi and Meza, splitting firewood with heavy steel axes. Bits of wood flew high as the axes fell upon the dry logs. The men's armpits released a strong odour which registered in their minds the heavy work they were doing. They continued finishing this log, then pulled in another from the monstrous pile that rose up like a mountain in the yard.

Outside, from a distance, the chief and the elders caught sight of a man pulling a goat by a tether which he clinched in his left hand while holding a whip in his right. All their eyes were stuck on the new-comer. He approached and sat on the pavement, his hand straining hard to pull the goat which was struggling to get loose. It was Mbembela. He greeted the chief and the elders, rendering profusely the many Anyalungu titles of the chief, and said that he had brought the tribe's lord some bit of relish. The chief, on his part, gabbled his thanks and pointed to Mbembela the direction of the backyard. Mbembela stood up and proceeded to the backyard, where Meza showed him the pen. He went to the pen and shut the goat there.

"Meza! " Gumwele called. Meza appeared.

"And what of the goat I told you to go and bring from *Jambe* Mihanyo at Mpunguta?" he roared at him.

"But I was splitting firewood in the backyard."

"But I can hear only one axe. Is Magadi not there?"

"He is there," Meza said, looking at blood coming from his right foot where he had wounded himself with the axe. "I wounded myself and I was not splitting after that." As they were talking, Mbembela appeared from the backyard. He was about to sit down when Sindege, one of the elders, called him to his side.

"Do you see that Meza is wounded? Look at him." The old Anyalungu fellow pointed at the red wound on the foot of Meza. "Now go into the compound and split the firewood for your chief. Go," Sindege said. Mbembela turned round and soon two axes were heard falling upon the dry logs.

Meza looked around the place and found a dirty bit of *kaniki* that was buried under the earth. He pulled the cloth out and used it to dress his wound. He went over and sat on the concrete pavement of the chief's car shelter. Flies came buzzing near the new wound and Meza was busy trapping them and occasionally crushing them between his palms, leaving red patches of blood on them.

The chief's face wrinkled with vague nervousness. He never talked much and only nodded when the elders tried to say this or that in the way of pricking his interest. At length the elders, too, realized the weary disinterestedness the chief hung over whatever they were eager to discuss. They chose to keep quiet also and bury themselves under their thoughts. The place maintained this tedious silence, interrupted only by the thundering of axes in the backyard. Then all turned their faces and their necks were bent in the direction of the road that came up from the town.

Mr Samuel drove in his new red car and the brakes squealed as he pulled up in the compound.

"Chief," he said, looking about searchingly, "I came to seek some help. I have had guests from Morogoro. They are my uncle and his cousin with their families. They have come with a lot of luggage."

"Who is this uncle?" Gumwele asked.

"Do you know Augustin? His home is just beyond the Ngaza church, on the right."

"Augustin," the chief murmured, trying hard to recall. "Ah! Augustin, he is a teacher, isn't he?"

"Yes, it is he. He is teaching in Morogoro and he has now come for the holidays. But his cousin with whom he has come is retiring and it is this cousin who has all that luggage."

"I see," Gumwele said, nodding.

"Now Chief, I want some people to carry that luggage." "Are there no people in the town?"

"By this time there is nobody anywhere. And I thought that I would find people here. Don't you have any?" Samuel said, looking about. He caught sight of Meza bending over his wound and his eyes never left him for sometime. "I don't need many people. Four or five will be enough. My uncle and his company will sleep here and I will take them there tomorrow in my car. But for the luggage, I want it to go there today."

"Kajanja . . ." Gumwele called and the driver of his land-rover appeared. "We want some people to carry out a little task. See if you can get any in the backyard."

Kajanja disappeared and in a minute he came out with Magadi, Mbembela, another visitor called Akusala and the cook.

"You go on with your cooking in the kitchen," Gumwele told the cook. "Meza is wounded. Now you, Kajanja, with Magadi and these other people," the chief pointed at Mbembela and Akusala, who just kept looking on without understanding, "go to the town. There I am sure you can get one person or two. Then, Kajanja, you can come back."

The small team started off immediately, those who understood as well as those who did not. Before reaching the town, Samuel passed them. He slowed down a bit and peeped out of the car window.

"Does any one of you know where my house is?" he asked them.

"Yes, I know it, *Bwana Mkubwa*," Magadi mumbled hastily.

"Then meet me there. Make haste" He finished this and drove off leaving them in a cloud of dust. The group walked on silently. They were then in the town when Magadi ordered the others to halt. He stood there for a minute or so gazing with an increased keenness all over the town streets, like a predator tracing the trail of an escaping prey. The streets, they found, were completely deserted. Magadi thought hard, turning round and round.

"This way, quick," he instructed the others. They rushed along the streets almost running. They first went down the street on the left and past the storeyed building of Khanji. Then Magadi gave a sudden jerk backwards. The others stopped too.

"You, there!" he yelled. "Come here," he addressed a man sitting on the pavement singing a lullaby and playing with a crying Indian child. Mbembela recognized him. It was Zayumba. Zayumba pretended that he did not hear what Magadi had said.

"Can't you hear? It is you I am talking to." Zayumba did not move. He only looked at them.

"I tell you to come," Magadi said again. He was already warmed up.

"Aaah, Magadi why do you solicit that much? Drag him. If he refuses then he will appear before the D.C. tomorrow," Kajanja yelled. That had been enough. Zayumba began to quiver. He had wanted to mutter something but then his mouth closed tight. Magadi counted with his left hand the three people who were to carry the loads. As Zayumbajjoined them Kajanja glimpsed somebody going up the street behind them and disappearing behind a building.

"This way, quick!" Magadi commended, running, and the whole team running behind him. When they reached the building behind which the fellow had disappeared they could see no trace of him. Magadi stood stupefied, his hands at his waist. He kept turning round and round like a hunting lion. Then he saw somebody sitting on the steps of the shop of Charan, his back to them, he wore a cloak with something red on the back.

"Come this way!" Magadi yelled again.

Lubele, who had been sitting outside waiting for Kamuyuga to finish his business with Charan, then turned round for the first time and saw that he was surrounded.

"You, here, come with us," Magadi spoke harshly. Lubele was stupefied. He couldn't comprehend all that he saw within that short time. The words only came to his ears very faintly. He just kept gazing at them. He saw Zayumba, Mbembela and the chief's messenger, Magadi, whom he recognized. There was no more to think about. He knew that it was for the case Kamuyuga had told him about in the morning. So Mbembela, he thought, had sent the case to the chief and now he was being arrested. So Kadufi had won at last. Lubele's heart throbbed loudly and he already began to suffer the punishment of gaol. That house he had dreaded all his life, then, would become his home.

"Can't you hear?" Magadi roared.

Lubele stood up, leaving his basket on the landing, and joined the group. Zayumba now forgot all his worries about himself and thought of the fate of his father-in-law. It pained him very acutely to see Lubele burdened with so much humility and particularly in front of a son-in-law. Spontaneously, he bent down and picked up the basket.

Inside the shop of Charan, Kamuyuga and Charan had been peeping. They saw all that was going on and Kamuyuga thought that he could comprehend the situation. He began narrating to Charan the whole story about Mbembela, Lubele, Mihanyo and everything about the case of Lubele, which Kamuyuga suspected was the main cause of Lubele's arrest in this manner by Magadi. But he wondered why Magadi did not have his handcuffs. Charan got very amused, particularly when he heard that the old fellow who sat outside his shop waiting for Kamuyuga, sent a cock to Jumbe Mihanyo and that the bribe became poison in his own blood. He laughed very much, showing all his cracked teeth and exposing even the molars. Kamuyuga was pleased to see that Charan could be so happy in his company. He exaggerated the affair further and further.

The small group of six people walked down the street hastily. Magadi and Kajanja walked behind, pushing the others in front of them. Four people would suffice, Magadi thought, and especially on a very unfortunate day such as this one, when he had to run about chasing people. He talked to Kajanja very gaily, making the only noise that came very faintly into the ears of the hapless group that walked before them. Lubele had dried up completely. The sight of Mbembela among the crowd crazed him with fear. They went on.

At the home of Mr Samuel, they were greeted by a loud noise blaring from a huge radio on a low table. Inside the house, too, were loud yells of children who climbed up the legs of the guests, disturbing the talk that went on. Watch them, Kajanja," Magadi instructed the chief's driver as he mounted the steps into the house. Not long after he reappeared.

"Come in, all of you," he shouted at those outside. They went in. The sitting room was messed up. The carpet was completely buried beneath a huge heap of the guests' luggage. The small cupboards, mattresses, suitcases, pillows, legs of beds, a sewing machine, and some other things wrapped in *khangas* all lay here and there.

"Alright, now," Samuel began, "each one of you has to carry as much as he can." Lubele carried a huge suitcase on his head and the two legs of the sewing machine on top of it. Others carried two suitcases one above the other. When they had loaded themselves with enough luggage they stood outside on the road. However, they did not carry everything. Some items still lay there. Samuel looked at the group outside that had the loads on their heads. Maybe that is enough for them, he thought.

"Magadi," he called. "you are not going?" Magadi turned, already suspecting the burden about to be placed upon him.

"The chief needs us back. Me and Kajanja, we have to split the firewood. That's why we made much haste in looking for these people" Magadi said, trying to avoid the eyes of Samuel.

"Alright. I think they have carried enough. But you, Magadi, if you want to avoid going to Ngaza then go and call Juma. Do you know Juma, that messenger in my office?"

"He lives at Majengo?"

"Yes, maybe. I'm not sure. Go and look for him. Hurry up."

Samuel was left there looking at the day's victims: "Put the loads down first. Are you to keep them on your heads until Magadi comes?" Augustin, the uncle of Samuel, asked them. They unloaded.

"Ah, don't worry yourself about them, Uncle," Samuel said "I know them. They carry bananas everyday on their heads. Loads far bigger than what you see them carrying now. And then the money, they finish all in drinking. They can stay at a beer party the whole night."

Augustin burst out laughing.

"True," Samuel continued. "Do you think that's a lie? And once they get themselves one shirt or so, or like that thing that old fellow is putting on, see," Samuel pointed at the cloak Lubele was wearing, "once they get themselves such a thing on their bodies and if they buy their wives one *kaniki* sheet, then it is over. *Pombe* all the time."

Ten minutes had elapsed when Magadi, accompanied by Juma, appeared from a dirty alley. Lubele looked at Juma. He recognized him. This Juma was *Baba* Athumani, the one who had married the niece of Kamuyuga.

Augustin went in and bent over the remaining load. Then he called Mr Samuel. "See," he said. "Not much is remaining. These two messengers could take some from here and also those outside could add a little more. We shall then be left with only a little which we would be able to carry tomorrow very easily." Samuel agreed to the plan. They came out.

"Magadi," Samuel called. "If you say that the chief needs you at home urgently, then I will give a chit to Kajanja and he will convey it to Gumwele, telling him that I have also needed you very much."

Magadi looked down without remark. He knew that he, too, had fallen into the work and that he could not escape. He lifted one bundle that had been tied in a *khanga* and *Baba* Athumani hauled another. They were going out when Augustin caught *Baba* Athumani by the arm and made him swing round.

"What now! Are you going to carry this small thing like a little child?" *Baba* Athumani took a suitcase. He put it on his head first and the other bundle came on top. Two chairs were given, one to Lubele and another to Akusala, who clasped them in their right arms. Augustin tossed two coins, one at Juma and another at Magadi. They were fifty-cent coins. Mr Samuel made a lot of fuss and he gesticulated wildly about the offer of the coins. He wanted them returned. The two messengers, too, shyly murmured something to protest the giving of the coins, while they slipped the coins into their pockets as if unconscious of doing so.

The group of six, staggering under the weight of the heavy loads on their heads, walked silently along the main street. As they neared the market somebody appeared from behind a street corner and ran headlong into the group. It was Kamuyuga. Magadi saw that now at last he could evade the long journey to Ngaza. He would catch this man and exchange places with him. His heart flashed with joy. He threw down his load as he yelled at Kamuyuga to come. Kamuyuga looked round and saw that there were no other people. He ran away, stumbling and many times almost falling. He ran towards the market, his white kanzu flopping in the wind. Magadi ran after him. Baba Athumani began to laugh very heartily. The others, Zayumba, Mbembela and Akusala, laughed very much, too, despite the heavy loads that were pressing down on them. It appeared to amuse them greatly to see Kamuyuga so much terrified. Only Lubele kept quiet. He was serious and sorry.

Charan, informed of what was taking place outside, left the hot embers where he had been warming himself. He came out and stood in front of his shop. Kamuyuga ran round the market building twice, and Magadi followed him. When he saw Kamuyuga run Charan laughed, very much amused. Magadi ran on and kept shouting names at Kamuyuga as the laughter of others became quite loud and some faces could be seen peeping out of windows. When Kamuyuga saw that Magadi was making fast upon him, he ran towards the the shop of Charan, where he thought he would take refuge. But when Charan saw that Kamuyuga was making in that direction, the shopkeeper ran inside and closed the door behind himself.

Kamuyuga then became desperate, but he still did not give up. He curved to the left and ran down the street. Magadi gave out some few yells and turned round to go back. He arrived where the others had stood with the loads waiting for him and found that the laughter still continued.

"*Shenzi sana,*" he cursed. "I would have caught him but you know why? It is because the street the fool chose passed outside the house of Bwana Samuel. Now I feared that Bwana Samuel would see me and what do you think he would say? He would know that I was unwilling to go to Ngaza," Magadi said as he picked up his load.

They resumed their march. Juma — *Baba* Athumani —walked in front, followed by Zayumba and the others, while Magadi walked last. They went in a single long line, keeping constant the distant between one another. Just past the office of the D.C., the *boma* as it was called, Juma halted. He had been to the home of Samuel at Ngaza more than twice and he knew the way there perfectly well.

"Hallo, Magadi," he called. "We have got to pick a shortcut and it is here." He pointed to a footpath on their right. "Otherwise by road via Mbazala Mission, it is eighteen miles." He did not wait for a reply. He stepped off the road and the others followed him along the narrow footpath which wound its way in the bush like a long snake. There was no noise besides the pattering of the bark-hard soles of their feet on the bare earth.

The wind had stopped blowing. It was calm and dark under the black clouds. Soon after, the massive drops began to shower heavily upon the overloaded peasants.

They marched on and on in the rain. Their wet clothes fitted them very tightly, showing all the feature of their bodies inch by inch. The loose cloak of Lubele which had formerly been swaying about in the wind now shrunk tight

to his body and the wet letters NANCY were rendered a deeper red colour. After two hours the rain ceased to fall. A thick mist closed in, making it even harder to see the surrounding vegetation some few metres away from the path. An hour or so later the mist cleared, leaving only isolated patches here and there.

They passed several homesteads that released smoke from their grass thatched roofs. On several occasions, just past or before passing these homesteads, they found goats tied to bushes, their hair clumped together like thorns, and no less wet than the vegetation around them. The poor animals kept looking at the passers-by, apparently wishing that they had come to rescue them from the ensuing darkness and cold. But to the goats' disappointment, each man passed without even noticing the animals. Still the goats kept looking with raised heads at the men, one by one, as if counting them.

It was about ten at night when the men arrived at Ngaza. They put down their monstrous loads and stood in the open yard of the house of Samuel. Their necks stayed bent despite the great effort with which each tried to stretch his. Lubele, now without the load on his head, felt like a coiled spring let loose to thrust up in the air. They stood there for a while until they realised that there was nothing that bound them to this place after handing over the loads. They broke off. Lubele, with his son-in-law, Zayumba, walked in front and later, on the way, they picked a short-cut on their left to Mpunguta and thence to Nlimanja. Mbembela, who feared to go with Lubele, chose to go with the others to town where he would pick his way anew to Mpunguta. They all vanished without much talk, in the bright rays of the moon.

ELEVEN

Early next morning, Mbembela walked into the compound of
Kadufi. Kadufi was already awake and had come out of the house
dressed in a bedsheet slung over his shoulder.

"Did you sleep well?" Kadufi enquired of his visitor.

"Aa, pains all over."

"And were you able to see him yesterday?"

"Yes, I went there and I presented the goat."

"But did the chief or someone mark your face?" Kadufi
enunciated his words very clearly. "Did he show any signs of
pleasure with you? I am asking it because this is what is important."

Mbembela looked doubtful. He couldn't answer straight away.
But the sharp eyes of Kadufi worried him. He hesitated and was
about to answer by explaining what had happened at the chief's,
detail by detail. But his tongue slipped and a "yes" came out. His
eyes shone.

Kadufi took his eyes off Mbembela and spoke, looking up in the blue sky as if addressing someone far off, in a low, painful tone.

"I have just awakened and I was about to come to your house," he said.

"Aaa?"

"Eeee. Because I had something to beg of you."

"What was it?"

"I will come to talk it over there at your house." "Alright, then you will meet me there."

"Yes," Kadufi spoke firmly and with a new liveliness, shaking off all the pain just expressed in his voice. "I am washing my face and I will come there immediately after that."

Mbembela walked out of the compound to his house. He went over to the cage of fowls and swung the tiny door. The fowls came out, making a lot of noise and heaping their refuse here and there in the yard. As he left the cage Kadufi arrived.

"Do you know that Lubele and Mihanyo nearly killed each other yesterday?" Kadufi began even before getting seated.

"No, I haven't heard anything."

"So Lubele came to learn that you are planning to send the case to the chief and even further."

"And who told him?" Mbembela screwed up his face, shocked.

"Why? That was no matter for a secret. Do you fear?"

"Oh, no," Mbembela said against his will, evading the cunning eyes of Kadufi. "I don't fear."

Kadufi went on, picking up a stick and drawing patterns on the soft, still-moist ground.

"Yesterday Andunje came to my house to call me. It was past midnight. I said, 'What is it, Andunje?' and he answered, 'Lubele is at the house of *Jumbe* Mihanyo, and the *jumbe* has sent me to call you, a court elder.' I tell you Andunje was panting. I asked him, 'And what does Lubele – want?' He answered, 'Lubele claims a cock — he says his cock. He has heard that the-case goes further to the chief and even to Bwana D.C., therefore he wants his cock back."

"Which cock is that?" Mbembela asked.

"Aaah? Do you forget the cock I told you was the bribe?"

"Ah, yes. And did you go?"

"I didn't. I told them openly that I was no longer court-elder and did not even share a feather when Mihanyo ate the cock. And I told them openly, too, that I don't involve myself with such infamous things like bribes."

Fear was seen in the eyes of Mbembela and Kadufi did not fail to notice it. He just went on drawing the patterns on the soil.

"Did you fear him?" Kadufi asked, with a weird look which made Mbembela quiver to his bowels.

"Fear whom?" he managed to ask.

"Lubuele or Mihanyo?"

"Aaaa, no! "Mbembela felt once more the awkwardness of that question which Kadufi kept putting before him again and again. He remembered that day of the quarrel and a cold shiver ran down his spine, giving his back more pain along the tracks of that hippo whip.

In the ensuing moments they sunk deep, each in his own thoughts. There was a silence except for the clucking of the chicks scattered all around. Then Kadufi broke the silence.

"I think I told you that I had a problem."

"Yes." Mbembela looked down, expecting something very grave.

"I have been sick all these two days. I have not been able to eat properly. This is because of *tajuni*. Everyday eating *tajuni* has made my stomach ache continuously. I want to borrow this one," Kadufi said, pointing at a big, fat hen that passed before them.

"My hen, that big one, is about to hatch. If it hatches successfully and when the chicks reach their full size, you will get your hen back," he finished hastily.

Mbembela did not say anything. Kadufi kept gazing at the hen. "How about it?" he asked,

"Which one?" Mbembela asked, without having thought of putting forth that question.

"This one."

Mbembela felt very reluctant. But he didn't want to show his feelings. When he understood that he could not trifle with the request just like that, without sowing a new thing that would grow poisonous to him, he leaped forth and fell upon the hen. Kadufi found nothing more to wait for. He stood up and grabbed the fowl from Mbembela.

"Now don't delay the thing," he said, looking solemnly at Mbembela. "If you wait longer it will be obstructed by Mihanyo or anybody else. It is fatal once Mihanyo has known that you passed him over."

Mbembela kept his silence and continued to draw lines on the ground with his big toe.

"Go there this very day," Kadufi added as he turned round and walked home.

It was about two o'clock when Mbembela came into sight of the glittering roof of Chief Gumwele's residence. He walked on and on, thinking deeply of the new thing Kadufi had brought to him. He envisaged a difficult future. How could he live there, at Mpunguta, near Lubele and Mihanyo? It worried him, too, to think of the type of friendship that Kadufi bestowed upon him. That weird look in his eyes particularly. They pierced him like a poisoned arrow whenever Kadufi looked at him.

As these thoughts sank deeper and deeper, Mbembela jerked back spontaneously. He wanted to return and forget all about the affair. There were more problems arising before him. A new thought occurred to him. He wanted to return and apologise to Mihanyo and Lubele and tell them that it was Kadufi who drove him, who designed all those evils. And if the apology would need something to go hand-in-hand with it, then he was ready for that, too.

But as his head tried hard to ponder over the matter the shadow of Kadufi came to him and hung very heavily over his soul. He shivered and started forth to the chief's court. He arrived. The chief was sleeping inside. It was hot and, as usual, the court elders sat along the verandah on huge armchairs. The two messengers, Meza and Magadi, sat at their sides on the level floor. Meza was busy with flies that came to feed on his wound. His palms struck against each other, crushing the flies between them, and the corpses fell accumulating at his ankles below.

As Mbembela swept into the compound the place livened a little with the sharp voice of Magadi, who loudly showered Mbembela with questions as he led him towards the chief's court.

"But Yakobo is not in the court office, he is in the backyard washing clothes," Meza shouted at them. Yakobo couldn't be in the court at any rate. There was nothing to write about and this clerk of the chief only worked as clerk one minute in a week, and as for the rest, he could as well be called a laundry man.

They halted. Magadi went into the backyard and called Yakobo, Magadi, with Mbembela in front of him like a prisoner, walked down to the court room with Yakobo coming behind them. In five minutes the summons was handed to Mbembela. As they came out of the court office the court elder, Sindege, was there at the door. Magadi and Yakobo retired to the palace.

Mbembela also started walking his way home and Sindege came trailing behind him.

"Son," Sindege called. Mbembela looked back. Sindege caught up with him. Then Mbembela turned and they stood facing each other. He had already started to suffer the misfortune he had been expecting.

"Aren't you the good son who came here yesterday?"

"Yes, it is."

"You came to get a summons, isn't it?

"Yes."

Sindege smiled forcefully and Mbembela read on the other man's face that unearthly look familiar from the face of Kadufi. Mbembela dried up and his throat parched.

"I remember you very well," Sindege continued, "I longed to visit you at your home one day but only that I didn't know where you live, my son."

Mbembela did not say anything. He kept his eyes down on the maize beds and burrowed his big toe in the loose sand. Sindege changed his tone into one of much affection.

"It appears that you have got a good stock at home. Yesterday, that one, that he-goat you brought the chief, was a great thing you did, my son. Only that you children forget that you have got your parent, Sindege, here. Is the chief living here alone? We are all living here, but do we share the same kitchen? Can't you say one day 'let me go to Baba Sindege and send him this or that'?" Sindege finished and anxiously waited to hear from Mbembela. Mbembela kept his eyes still fixed on the ground, his body tense and his manner servile.

"I expect a present from you, a present from my son," Sindege continued to press hard. When he saw that he was very unlikely to win anything from Mbembela, he screwed up his face and it wrinkled with seriousness.

"If you are that much mean, my son, you won't win the case. It is me who is the chief's court, and the chief's court is Sindege. If you want to win the case, tomorrow come to my house there." Sindege pointed at a mud house far from the compound of the chief. "As for me, I don't need a goat as big as that one you sent the chief yesterday, no. Just a sizeable one, I don't mind. But if even that you can't give then I promise you that you will come to know who Sindege is." Finishing this Sindege walked back, leaving Mbembela still drawing patterns on the beds. When Sindege disappeared Mbembela started off homewards.

It was almost dark when he reached home. He stood outside the house thinking. He felt himself a stranger. Mpunguta, that place where his fathers had lived, the place where he had been born and brought up, married and enjoyed life, was now somehow unfamiliar to him. He looked like a newborn baby without parents or guardians. He began thinking of his divorced wife. He brought out the chit he had received from Yakobo and let his fingers feel it again and again. The face of Sindege came to him. It faded and the uncanny expression on the face of Kadufi took its place.

Mbembela went over to the pen and looked at his animals. They looked as sad and humble as himself. He went across the yard to the cage of fowls. He pulled the tiny door and peeped at the birds clustering together inside. He turned round hastily, afraid. He was shaking with fear. His mind had registered the presence of Kadufi. And in the stillness of the darkness, like a ghost, Kadufi stood behind him.

"Did you go?"

"Yes, I went," Mbembela replied unwillingly.

"Did you get it?"

"Yes"

"I just came to check. Go just now and give it to Lubele." As he finished this Kadufi disappeared in the darkness.

Mbembela felt his legs yield under him. The whole affair seemed too heavy for him. Could he approach Lubele? No, he decided at last. His fingers tightened and the chit which was the summons tore into pieces and scattered before the hen's cage in the courtyard. He went over to the pen again and tied loops around the necks of the three animals, went into the house and fetched a basket in which he put a shuka, a khaki pair of shorts, two big tin bakulis, a tray, two cooking pots and a stick.

That was all his property.

Half an hour later, Mbembela had the basket that carried his belongings on his head and in his right hand he gripped the tethers that held the goats by the necks. On his left hand was a big nest consisting of his one cock and three hens. He was marching away from his home. Twenty metres off he halted. He gazed at the house for a few minutes. In this short time Mbembela's past life flashed before his mind. His deeds, good and bad. Tears stood in his eyes and he swung round at last, his eyes registering the Mpunguta hills rising up in the dark sky. He seemed to see beyond them. He could see Mkomolo, the home of his uncles and cousins. A place of refuge for his troubled and humiliated soul, he thought, as he picked his way along the route leading to Mkomolo.

TWELVE

Dawn fell upon Mbazala Mission. Dew lay everywhere, on the tall steeple, on the creeping grass of the mission compounds, on the leaves of the tall cone-tree that surrounded it, everywhere. It was chilly. Two hundred metres away from, the mission house lay the Mbazala Boys' Boarding Middle School.

The brightening eastern horizon sent faint light falling upon the plain. The light made it possible to distinguish one building from the other at first, then gradually even one brick from another. Faint rays fell upon the old wooden door, the short verandah leading to the head teacher's office, the huge motor-car tyre ring that served as a bell hanging on its pole, the football field. At length even the single grains of sand could be identified. The day had commenced.

But the wooden windows which closed tight in their frames gave no sign of the oncoming daylight. In one of the dorms, on a bed in the corner, somebody awoke abruptly. He listened for a while to the breathing of his fellow boarders sleeping in the dorm. They slept soundly like little babies. He envied them.

Throwing off his blanket he got out of his bed, dressed, and went over to the window. He pulled the bolt. Strong sunlight dazzled his sleepy eyes. The outside had awakened some time ago, he discovered. His heart throbbed. Without wasting more time he rushed to the door and ran out. The light, which was growing more and more intense, worried him and he ran the two hundred metres to the church, mounted the steps and opened a small side door that led up to the steeple. He climbed the cold steps, breathlessly making his way up. The pattering of his footsteps ceased and the bell started ringing, sending a familiar note without interference across the plains and ridges. It rang for half a minute or so, then the sound of the huge bell was slowly swallowed by the chilly morning air.

The whole dorm, plus those nearby, awoke, and the school boys streamed hurriedly to the church. Believers from the neighbourhood, teachers and students entered the church and sat in their places in orderly fashion. The Reverend Father Waters said the mass.

Half an hour later the boys took their breakfast, hot gruel. They sat at long tables stretching right across the dining room. At the end of one table sat a boy wearing a red sweater over his khaki uniform shirt, white stockings and polished black leather shoes. He cut a piece of bread from a small bag by one of the table legs. He dipped a knife in a tin of margarine that lay on the table and carefully smeared margarine on the bread. He passed it aside to a friend sitting opposite him, bending over his own bowl of hot gruel.

"Take this, Simon," he said. The other boys squinted rapidly at the buttered piece of bread that Simon received. They returned their now-blank eyes to their gruel.

A massive iron going fell several times on the steel tyre ring in the school compound, sending familiar notes to the boys in the dining room. They left their clean bowls at their bedsides and rushed out. They lined up on the quadrangle in three rows, standard eight on one end and standard five on the other. They stood with their arms at their sides waiting anxiously for the headteacher, Mr George Manono, to make his appearance. In front of the anxious boys a group that made the school band had lined up, too. The drummers stood in front; those with flutes, at the back, whistling softly. At last the headteacher appeared, followed by Ezekiel Mayenge, assistant headteacher. These two walked stiffly and stood before the pupils.

"Today we will go on with the work we started the day-before-yesterday. Five will remove all spider webs on the walls of the whole school. Seven will deck the dorms. Eight will wash the classroom desks and six will wait here. Those already assigned can go to their places of work."

The boys dispersed. Then Mr Manono turned to go back to his office, when he remembered something.

"Boys, a moment," he said turning round. Mr Mayenge's went over to the bell and it sounded again. The boys ran back to their lines and the place resumed its orderly peacefulness. Mr Manono took a note out of his pocket. He glanced up and caught the eyes that kept looking at him attentively.

"The following should remain outside my office: John Bayike, Joseph Mkoe, Simon Lubele, and Alphonce Chobwe." As he finished saying this, the two teachers marched away and the boys scattered, leaving standard six standing in place.

The boys whose names had been mentioned followed and waited outside Mr Manono's office, along the short verandah. Mr Mayenge's voice was heard calling, "John Bayike." John Bayike, a youth of twenty-one, entered. That year he was in standard eight, final year at Mbazala before joining one of the two institutions in the districts, Ngaza Seminary or Ngaza Teachers Training College. Both of these were under the missionaries.

Simon Lubele walked the whole length of the short verandah and then halted to lean against the wall. There were a lot of things going on in his head. Probably they were calling him on fee problems. But, no, not that, he thought. He had settled that problem a year ago with Mr Mayenge. He would be giving half the amount, which by then he had already given three days ago when school re-opened.

His eyes were fixed on the floor for a long time and he went over past events in a rush. At Easter-time two years before, Mr

Nyalo, his former teacher at Mpunguta Bush School, who was then very close to the Lubeles, appeared at their home at Nlimanja.

He had brought with him an old friend who had been with him at Ngaza Teachers Training College. This fellow he introduced as Mr. Mayenge. Lubele had prepared some beer and a chicken for the guests. The two teachers enjoyed themselves as they talked and ate.

"Simon," Mr. Nyalo had called him, "what do you do at home nowadays?" Before Simon had been able to answer, his father took over.

"He is doing nothing." The old man had been a bit too straightforward, thought Mayenge, who had by then gathered interest in the boy.

He asked his friend in English. "Has he been your pupil?"

"He has been my pupil, a bright boy," Nyalo said in Anyalungu, patting Simon on his back fondly. "Father, how about sending him to middle school at Mbazala?" he said, looking at Lubele directly in the face. Lubele kept quiet. But it was obvious he wanted to speak out about something. It never came out, except that what he was feeling was to be read on his face. His whole countenance darkened.

"Because my parents have not been baptized, I couldn't get admission," Simon explained, with childish frankness.

The two teachers did not remark. It was something they knew quite well. They and those few before them had the same obstacles to go through. Moreover they were themselves the executors.

They had lived within a strong missionary influence which had bred deep in them pessimism and ill-will towards those who stood their ground against foreign customs.

They themselves had swallowed the foreigners' doctrine and it flourished in their minds. But they were tortured by the thought that they had turned out to be their own executioners, by nursing their alignment with their foreign masters and exercising a strong ill-will against their own people. Those were but the people by whom they had been brought up. Those very people were the ones who shared their problems, people of their day-to-day life. The two teachers felt sandwiched. They looked at the father and son for a longtime and the battle that was fought everyday in their souls started up again then, with even more vigour. There was a pitiful air, an air of having borne all the oppression of the period bit by bit, on the face of Lubele. Lubele's pathos weighed heavily on the hearts of the two teachers. Nevertheless there was also on the man's face a confidence that had never lost its freshness. And this, too, disturbed the hearts of the two teachers. On the face of the son, there was that innocence typical of childhood but it seemed to camouflage a spirit which would definitely challenge the present state of affairs sooner or later. This indefinable, elusive quality of the boy was now obscure, but it could be only accumulating force. These possibilities somehow threatened the teachers even more.

"Don't you think you could try to fix this one at your school?" Mr Nyalo had asked his friend. "They are very good people. You could help them," Nyalo added in English.

"I could do so, but it is difficult. But I will try my best. You know that father-in-charge, the Reverend Waters, is not so strict as he was when we were his pupils. You remember?"

"Aah! Those days he was too ridiculous," Nyalo said, laughing. "But you could just cheat that the boy's parents are baptised and all could end well. Is that not possible?"

"Well, wait and I will see if it is possible or otherwise."

Thus Simon Lubele was registered the year before at Mbazala Boys'. Joseph Mkoe, a standard seven boy, entered the head-teacher's office as John Bayike came out. Not much time elapsed before Joseph came out and Simon was called in. There was one thing he was anticipating as the cause of his being summoned. It was about his fathers's paganism. The thought broke the heart of the boy and he entered the office feeling already defeated.

Opposite the headteacher sat Mr Mayenge, smiling Simon stood near the table, his arms at his sides and his feet close together. His heart throbbed loudly.

"Simon," Manono called.

"Yes, sir."

"At what time do you wake up when it is your turn to ring the church bell?" Simon did not answer immediately. He cast his eyes to the floor as if trying to think.

"I don't know the exact time, sir. We only wake early and when we enter the church, it is the church clock which tells us the time to ring," he managed to answer, but not without shaking. Mr. Mayenge looked at him all the while, not noticing the shaking of the boy's limbs.

"They tell time by cock-crow," Mayenge said.

The headteacher lifted his eyes. "You were late to ring the bell today."

"Yes, sir. Nowadays dawn comes a bit late."

Mr Manono kept playing with the pen in his fingers. He thought of the reply Simon had given and remembered the lesson he had prepared to teach standard eight. First lesson it was. The topic was "Day and Night". He looked at Simon again and he couldn't help admiring that the boy was very observant, though of course he had not accurately explained the phenomenon.

"Father Waters complained about this," Manono concluded, then went on.

"We have appointed you a prefect. You will be in charge of standard six."

"Yes, sir."

"Now take your class and go into the mission compound where you will meet somebody to show you work to do."

"Yes, sir."

"Go, and be careful about the bell for the morning mass."

Simon went out. He walked to the quadrangle still doubting that he had not been asked about his father's faith. By the time Simon came out of Mr Manono's office every pupil knew that he was one of the prefects. He announced the assignment for standard six and they started moving towards the mission house.

The boy in the red sweater caught up with Simon Lubele.

"What was it all about in Mr. Manono's?" he asked Simon.

"Nothing, except that I'm a prefect. That's all."

At the mission house they found the Reverend Father Waters waiting for them. He was a tall, slender man with blue eyes. That day he had had a haircut and he looked much younger than he actually was. In front of him lay slashers and jembes. Simon looked at the Reverend with a thumping heart. He remembered the morning bell and thought that the Father would ask him about it.

All the boys came behind Simon and they gathered before Father Waters. Simon fell on his knees and almost instantly all did the same.

"Praised be Jesus Christ, good morning, Father," they said. Fathers Waters smiled broadly and beckoned them to stand up. He moved two steps forward and put his palm fondly on the head of the boy wearing the red sweater. The other boys watched. Father Waters looked at the boy full in the face as he bent forward a little.

"You are Samuel?"

"Willie Samuel, Father."

"Oh, yes. That's it. I haven't seen you for the past three days since the school re-opened. Don't you attend mass?"

"I came here only yesterday."

"Why, Willie?"

"My father's car was at the mechanic's and there was no transport for me."

"Now how did you come here? Did you walk?"

"No. Father brought me yesterday."

"Did your father come here yesterday? Why did he not come to see me?" the Reverend said, stretching himself up again. The other boys just kept looking on.

"It was late. About eight o'clock in the evening," Willie continued.

"When will he come again?"

"He will come today. That's what he told me."

"When he comes, tell him to see me, you hear,"

"Yes, Father." Then Father Waters looked at the other boys.

"Take the tools, boys, and you will remove all the grass in the compound." He patted Willie very affectionately and let him go. The boys dispersed and Father Waters disappeared into the mission house.

There was something shared by the countenances of all the boys, something different from the expression on the face of Willie. Willie had happiness all over him. His face had brightened completely and his very being exuded contentment. He walked towards his comrades but nobody looked at him. Once or twice he tried to say something but there wasn't a remark from anybody. There was something eating very deep in the hearts of the boys.

Each one of them felt sorry for himself. Each felt worthless. Why were their fathers not chief clerks like Willie's? Every one of them wished to be treated the way Willie was. Everyone wished to be valued and loved by fellow pupils, teachers and even priests, to be driven to school in a car, to wear a sweater over school uniform without reprimand from teachers, to eat bread smeared with magarine and wear shoes. The boys knew, too, that there were other intangible benefits occurring to one who had these things at hand.

More than just feeling how sickening the whole matter was to them and all their compatriots, the boys could never define what was the reason for such stark differences in social status. The injustice lingered heavily upon them, pressing their souls down and down.

These sentiments were brief and sharp, and once again everybody recovered, for such feelings occurred all their lives and were relatively inhibited. They were feelings none of them was prepared to let people find in him. Each tried to suppress them whenever he saw them erupt from their dark corner.

Willie went over to Simon. They talked as they worked. Willie told Simon many things, about Father Waters particularly about the way he associated with his father, the chance he would be given to go and study in Europe and the unlikelihood of his being able to accept because he had asthma, and so on. Simon listened with little interest, only occasionally nodding in assent. There were gradually lenghthening breaks where the two boys stopped working and talked, particularly Willie, as he stressed the various points in his endless narrative.

Then one boy called Mangangala began.

"Willie, you are only idling. Come and work. You are not a prefect."

"Shut up!" Willie frowned

"Shut up what? I won't."

"Then I will beat you up. Bush dog. You call yourself Mangangalason. Do you know what son means? Son is not for you."

The other boys cheered at this outburst, very much amused. They jeered and shouted, "Mangangalason, Mangangalason." Mangangala, a large youth of about nineteen years old, got hot. He found this making fun of his name one of the greatest insults.

"Now, if you think that you can fight me, come. You are very proud. You failed in your standard four exam, everybody knows. You don't have anything in your head and you thought that you would be appointed prefect," Mangangala sent it back to him. The two boys came close.

"Put down your slashers," the other boys shouted at them. Simon, conscious of being the prefect and a friend of Willie, grabbed the arms of Willie.

"Please, Willie. Don't, please," he coaxed him.

"No. Let me thrash this bush-boy," Willie mumbled, freeing himself from the bony grip Simon had on his arms. He went over and slapped Mangangala on the left cheek. All the other pupils laughed with great amusement, and taunted Mangangala. Mangangala, cursing in Anyalungu, grabbed the feeble arms of Willie and sent him staggering back. Willie tried to resist the push, but he fell when his ankles hit a flower bush.

Before anybody had comprehended fully what had happened, Father Waters arrived at the scene. His whole person vibrated with shock. He walked towards Willie and lifted him up. He examined him thoroughly and found that he was not bruised. The other boys had immediately gone off in different directions, all pretending to be working hard. Father Waters was shaking all over. There were drops of perspiration on his forehead and nose.

"Monitor, is there no monitor or prefect here?" he asked, holding Willie to his side. Simon came forth.

"Come to my office, with you, there," the Reverend said, pointing to Mangangala. Still holding Willie, he mounted the steps into the building, followed by Simon, with Mangangala coming last.

Father Waters sat at his desk.

"I have seen all that has happened," the Reverend said, with so much anger that the words did not come out clearly. Then he took a long, wild look at Mangangala.

"Why did you beat him? Don't you know that the child has asthma?"

Mangangala quivered. He went down on his knees. "I ask for your pardon, Father."

The Reverend's look of ferociousness changed suddenly to one of deep affection when he turned to Willie. "Are you hurt, Willie?"

"No," the boy replied, in the tone of a child much younger. The Reverend hugged him even more tightly now. He glared at Mangangala again.

"Stand up. I will send you out of school."

Mangangala remained on his knees. "I beg your pardon Father," he implored desperately. The Reverend pulled a drawer to his right and brought out a notebook and pen. He wrote:-

Manono,

This boy has brutally beaten Willie, knowing that the boy has asthma. If I had not been around, I can't say what would have happened. I'm very sorry for this and I'm afraid his father will be very sorry, too. How is this, Manono? Don't you teach these boys to behave? I always stress this thing to you — obedience.

I hope that I won't hear of any such thing again and you will impose a good deterring punishment.

Jones Waters

The Reverend tore off this page, folded it neatly and handed it to Mangangala.

"And what is your name?"

"Andrea Mangangala, Father."

Waters wrote this name on the pad and a note on it. "Take this to Manono. Then this evening before we gather for the evening mass, you should be in the church. Pray that God should forgive you. And you, monitor, see that Willie goes straight to bed. He shouldn't do any work the whole week.

"Yes, Father."

Mr Manono read the letter in silence and raised his head to eye Mangangala. He put down the letter and looked at Willie.

"When did you say your father would come again?"

"He said he would come this afternoon, after work," Willie replied, on a note of rising hysteria.

"When he comes, tell him that I would like a lift to town."

"Yes." Simon noted that Willie never said 'yes, sir,' like the other boys did and the teachers never said anything about it.

Mr Manono went on perusing the letter a while longer. Then he reached for the handle of a drawer to his right. He brought out a big book with thick covers labeled "BLACK BOOK." He wrote something in it, closed it and replaced it in the drawer. He reached for a long stick in the corner and stood up, brandishing it.

"Come near."

Mangangala came closer.

"Lie on the chair."

The boy did so. Mr Manono thrashed him on the buttocks twenty times. Tears dripped from the reddened eyesockets of Mangangala. He uttered no noise.

Mangangala marched out and disappeared into the dormitory. He could not sit, for his buttocks were burning. He leaned against the wall of the dorm near the door. His red eyes kept gazing blankly at the brown bricks on the wall of the dining room. Simon, with Willie preceding him, came into the dorm. The red sweater Willie wore never seemed to catch the eyes of Mangangala. Willie walked to his bed and Simon came over to spread the sheets over him. He left Willie there and retired to the mission house.

Mangangala stood there for twenty minutes without moving a limb. Then, almost unconsciously he moved into the dorm. He sat on his bed and bent down over his small wooden box where there were his belongings — some torn past years' uniforms, a toothbrush, some exercise books, two shillings in ten-cent coins and some few letters. He took one of the letters, one he had received only the day before, and read it slowly. He got stuck at one paragraph and read through this several times.

"I am even more sick than what you left me. I can't eat anything. Yesterday it extended to headache. I try with the herbs your aunt brought me but only little better. There is nobody at home. Your mother goes to till the shamba and I stay alone. About the school fees you said that I could negotiate with Father Waters. At the present moment I have not got a penny. If you think the way I do, come home and take a wife. You have already spent much time in school. Your age-mates Bosco and Manja have all taken wives."

Mangangala read that paragraph over and over. No, he wouldn't think the way his father did. He began thinking of the Reverend Father Waters. He thought, would the clergyman pity him if he explained his situation? It also came to him that his father had been a faithful follower of the white man's religion. Did he not deserve anything from them?

That afternoon Mangangala went to the mission house. He passed the gate and went straight into Father Waters' office. The Reverend was seated behind his desk as usual. Mangangala fell upon his knees.

"Praised be Jesus Christ! Good afternoon, Father." The Reverend kept quiet for a long while, turning the pages of a book over and over. At last he lifted his eyes towards the boy, who was only visible by his head, which projected above the desk.

"What do you want?"

"I have come to bargain my school fees. My father is very old and sick. He cannot pay."

"You are Andrea Mangangala?" Father Waters read the name on the notebook that lay on his desk.

"Yes, Father." Mangangala replied, still kneeling. The Reverend shook his head.

"Go away, I can't do anything."

At nine o'clock that evening, Simon strolled along the bedsides for the nine o'clock bed-check. He had to do the bed-check himself first before Mr Mayenge came to do it. One bed was lacking its owner. The bed had no, sheets or pillow either. Andrea Mangangala was not there.

THIRTEEN

A light wind blew over the town, picking up scraps of paper in its current, wherever they drifted up to the red walls of the mud houses. It was cold and the market was becoming less and less peopled. Music blared from the huge radios in the Indian shops, their usual Gujerati music being in full tide.

Charan sat in his shop on the big armchair, his legs resting apart on the counter and his right palm holding his cheek. Three years had elapsed since he came to Bulembe. Business was good, but not as he had expected. He was deep in thought when, like shadows, two women dressed in *kaniki* entered and stood before the counter.

"Match-boxes we want," they said, holding coins in their hands. Charan looked at them blankly. He shook his head. The customers looked at him for a while with discernible embarrassment on their faces. They looked at the matchboxes that lay on the shelf behind the shopowner, and then at him again. But he just seemed too deep in his world of dreams to be pricked to conscious attention by any gestures. They turned their backs on him and vanished.

"Alli," Charan called, without a single motion other than that of his lips. Alli appeared.

"Bring my sweater." Alli went into the bedroom and brought out a thick woolen sweater.

"Close the shop. I am going to Jayandra."

He went out to his second-hand land-rover, drove across the market square to a shop opposite his and parked at the roadside. He mounted the steps to the door of the shop.

There was a line of customers, some African women purchasing their needs. Charan passed through the counter by way of a side opening. Jayandra, who had then been serving the women, called for a servant to bring a chair. A big armchair was brought. Charan seated himself.

Jayandra, too, sat down, and engaged himself with his visitor. The women opposite the counter kept standing where they had been, still gripping their coins in their hands. They were anxious to be served and leave. They had been at the market since morning and were now tired and hungry. The sky was cloudy and soon it would rain. They kept gazing at Charan and Jayandra, watching their lips move up and down as if they understood and were interested in what was talked about, while the two shopkeepers engaged themselves in hearty conversation.

Then one of the women asked if she could get kerosene. Her voice was absorbed completely by the cold air without in the least disturbing the talk of the shopkeepers. Finally, one by one, the customers, burning with indignation, went away.

A vessel cut out of a kerosene *debe* was filled with hot embers and laid between Jayandra and Charan by a servant.

"Bring tea," Jayandra ordered the servant. The servant disappeared and in a quarter of an hour reappeared with a tray of cups and a kettle. Charan and Jayandra drank and talked, feeling the warmth which seeped through their pull-over sweaters deep into the marrow of their bones.

"This place is really cold."

"It's June. All the three months. May, June and July. You know Bulembe is on a plateau."

"Mmmh! It's cold, really," Charan insisted, bending a little more over the fire.

"But do you mind very much staying here? I mean, don't you like this place?"

"Bulembe is excellent," Charan said with a nod. Jayandra did not add anything and a silence reigned for a while. He kept looking blankly at the red embers and stretched his arms over the fire. It had begun to rain outside and water flowing in sheets coloured red by the bare earth streamed to fill the trenches at the roadsides.

"This place is quiet, too," Charan added.

"Yes, this place is quiet, food very cheap, and have you ever had any fuss with anybody among those at the boma?"

"Who?" Charan lifted his eyes to Jayandra.

Jayandra lifted his hands above his head to show the caps the messengers used to wear. "I mean messengers."

"Only once I had a little trouble with them, but only a little trouble, that year when I was still a stranger here. Alli, you know that servant I have, that Alli?"

"Yes. Tall and strong, with a big nose."

"That's him."

"He has on the face smallpox scars?"

"It is him. So, one, day I asked him to buy bananas at the market. Then you know how matters go with those constables, police, I can't know what they are actually."

"Aah! They are messengers but they turn out to be the police when it comes."

"So it is one of them. He caught Alli just before entering the shop with the bananas. I was there behind the counter and I saw it all happen."

The servant of Jayandra came in and fetched the utensils from the counter. Charan watched him do so, but did not stop the narrative.

"I was really surprised to see that Alli was completely possessed by fear. The messenger asked Alli about *kodi ya kichwa*. Alli became dumb, I tell you. He couldn't speak. 'Follow me' he told Alli. Alli asked him permission to go and put down the bananas in the shop first."

"Did he let him loose?"

"Ah! Let him loose? How? He agreed, but followed him into the shop."

"Eeehe."

"I stood looking at both of them. Alli entered first and the messenger second. He stood before the counter facing me. *'Abali gani, bana kuba. 1i boi ako, bana kuba?'*

"I said, *'Diyo, ii boi agu.'* He kept quiet and scrutinized the customers in my shop. Alli came back and stood in front of the messenger. The messenger kept looking at him and then fixed his eyes on me and said, *'Basi kwa kua ii ni boi a bana kuba.'*"

"And what did you do all this while he had been gazing at you?"

"I only smiled. The messenger kept looking at me for a while and turned to go. When he reached the doorsteps he stopped and leaned against the wall. When one of the customers went out of the shop, he fell on him and dragged him away."

Jayandra smiled happily and his whole body was charmed. "You did wrong."

"Wrong?"

"Yes, a great wrong. When he looked at your face as he said *'boi ako bana kuba,'* you would have tossed something at him."

"What thing?"

"Anything, some cigarettes, coins, anything. What do you think they subsist by? Something here, another there, that's the way they live."

"Actually there is something I can't understand about them. I can't understand their behaviour," Charan said, knitting his brow.

"Ah, the D.C. has given them powers of a tiger. But they don't get a good pay to attain a position equivalent to the rank of that power. So they behave like children. They are harsh to this person and at the same time humble to another. When they find somebody who is likely to give them some bit or other they become lambs. I have stayed here for ten years now, still I have had no quarrels with any of them. Even the clerks sitting in the *boma*. When I go there you hear *'Shikamoo, shikamoo,'* here and there." Jayandra said these last words lifting his head to eye his comrade. There was no remark from Charan. Jayandra continued.

"What about your business? That other day you complained about business or something."

"I wanted to ask your opinion. You know I want to establish smaller retail shops in the countryside because it seems that the competition is high here in the town."

Jayandra sat up in his chair and stretched his hand to reach one of the shelves. He fetched a knife and with it poked the fading embers.

"What I would advise you is to employ some African whom you can trust. Give him the goods and let him sell in the village. Each end of the month he should present the money to you."

"I have got one African. He lives over there, beyond the horizon somewhere in the bush. I can't locate exactly."

"But make sure that he is honest."

"I am sure he is, because whenever my wife or anybody in my house tells him to bring vegetables or something or other he comes early on the morning he is told."

"Also, he must not be foolish, or too quiet or have something of dullness. You know what a man of business should be. He must also know how to count coins."

"I am sure that man knows. He looks clever, and keen also."

"But he should not be *too* clever. That is a disadvantage to matter too."

Charan lifted his eyes and peered out. He reckoned that darkness would fall not long after then. He stood to go. "How," Jayandra muttered, astonished.

"It will get dark soon. I am going."

"But I had sent for you. How, now? We haven't dealt with the matter and you want to go."

Charan recoiled slowly and seated himself on the armchair again. There was an expression of anxiety on his face. His eyes stretched to their full size and his mouth widened towards the left.

"You say you sent for me?"

"Yes. You mean — what do you mean?"

"Who did you send to call me?"

Jayandra did not say anything. He raised himself and fetched the knife he had used to poke the embers before and made it again serve the new use he had discovered for it. There were only ashes remaining. He tossed the knife back onto its shelf and shouted the name of the servant in a coarse voice livid with anger, sending the name clattering into the little kitchen. The servant came out in a hurry and stood like a statue before his master.

"Bring us some more embers." His voice had now changed to express the totality of his indignation. The servant reappeared, bringing with him the red embers; that seemed to change Jayandra into a cooled man again.

"Didn't I send you to Mr Charan in the morning?"

The servant stood amazed. "You did."

"Did you go?"

"I met Alli at the market and I asked him to convey the message."

"But Alli never told me anything," Charan pleaded.

"Why did you tell Alli and not go yourself?" There was no reply. Jayandra pushed his armchair backwards a bit, escaping the heat that seemed about to burn his skin. In the meantime the servant stole out and back to the kitchen.

"These servants want to be served. They don't realize that they are to serve and not to be served. This is the case even with that punk, Alli. Many times I have noticed."

"It is easy to deal with them. Threaten to dismiss. They just can't risk their jobs. You know most of these people long to live in the town. They take up service for whatever you offer them. Just do so. Ah, it won't take a day before you get another."

"So I will tell Alli to quit. If he thinks he can live in the bush like what their cousins do, it makes no problem to me."

"You know, this Alli, I wanted to dismiss him quite long ago. He is not a fellow one can like. Always dirty, and in that same state he plays with my children. He has a lot of lice on his head and clothes. Last year I even offered my own shirt. But surprisingly he never put it on and since that day I have lost sight of it completely."

"These creatures," Jayandra now spoke with a gesture of both his arms, "these creatures, you seem not to understand them. How do you expect them to put on good clothes if they are not used to good things all their lives? He might have sold it or most probably his cousins have snatched it away from him. They are like that."

Darkness had by then overtaken the better part of the surroundings and the two shopkeepers could only see each other's eyes glittering in the faint light of the fire. There was a strange uneasiness between them. Charan expected some kind of surprise, while Jayandra seemed to fear the reaction his words might produce on his colleague.

They tried to bring into the conversation various topics which, as they both knew, were of little relevance.

At last Jayandra broke in, "I want you to help me." His voice had totally changed, so that when Charan heard these words he felt the strange sensation that a new person had been introduced into the house. Jayandra continued, "But this is also of some benefit to you, too."

"What is it?" The heart of Charan began to thump.

"You are still a stranger to Bulembe. But at least you can understand some of the things that are going on." Charan kept quiet, his eyes on the fire. He seemed to anticipate all that Jayandra was going to say and wished he could tell in a single word and let the thing go once and for all.

"Do you know that fellow called Samuel, that chief clerk?"

"Yes, I know him."

"He used to be a great friend of mine. Sometimes he used to come here and would take sugar, kerosene, whatever he liked. All smiles everywhere."

"And what now?"

"Wait and listen. You have been going to meetings with some people, at the house of Khanji. We talked about this that other day that we should hate this Khanji but you went there yesterday. This I have heard and seen. When you were entering the house of Khanji, you turned round to have a glance at my shop to see if I saw you. I had purposely closed it and I was peeping through my bedroom window."

Jayandra looked deep into the eyes of Charan and he thought he could read in them the whole truth of the affair.

"You know they came to call me, and I thought I couldn't . . ."

"O.K. As for this, I don't mind. You can choose between your countryman and other things. If you now want to abandon me, the man of your religion, the man of your country, me who received you in Bulembe and want to align yourself with Khanji because he is rich, because he owns a transport company, this is all up to you. You forget, Charan, that I have been loving you like a young brother all the time?"

Charan kept his eyes fixed on the ashes, his mouth absolutely shut.

"Last year, we had a meeting. That meeting you also, attended. I hope you remember. It was agreed upon raising the price of certain items. Sugar, we said, instead of fifty cents per half pound, should be eighty cents. From that meeting that was the new price. There is one thing I dislike. These Khanjis want to dominate everything, everybody. At any time you go to their shops, you find them filled. Our shops, do they not need customers? You know that this Khanji is very clever. When you all agree to raise prices, he doesn't. All shopowners of Bulembe, and you, too, want to become among this group. You all fear him, and he feels kingly. At what price did you sell sugar after that meeting?"

"Eighty cents," Charan answered in a voice hardly coming out.

"I sold at fifty and all the stock dried up the next day." Jayandra spoke defiantly. "I wanted Khanji to feel wounded and I enjoyed this. And it is for this thing that he started planning vengeance upon me."

"Vengeance, how?" Charan asked, this time with some energy in his voice.

"He has spent quite a big sum of money already, don't you know? Up to the moment . . ." Jayandra, at this point slackened his voice and cast his eyes thoroughly everywhere around before going on, "up to this moment Khanii is running his business without any taxes or licenc.se."

"Why?"

"Eeeh! You seem to arrive today in Bulembe. Haven't I talked to you of Samuel?"

"You have. But what has it to do with him?"

"You know that he has bought a car, a red car?"

"I have seen it many times."

"So three quarters of the price, Khanji gave out of his pocket. There are so many things that go on between these two. Me, too. I hadn't been paying all taxes. Until this year when, wonderfully, Samuel has changed his attitude towards me. I know it is because,of Khanji, he has influenced him to dislike me."

Charan did not r mark. He kept bending upon the fire, supporting his fists on his thighs. Jayandra continued.

"Now, tell me. What did you discuss at the meeting esterday?"

Charan did not answer immediately. He sat up and caught the eyes of Jayandra, which then shone with a light that appeared to spellbind him.

"Khanji said that nobody should cooperate with you. If anybody will do so then he will be an enemy of all the shop-owners of Bulembe. He added that he will not transport anything that belongs to any such person." Charan finished speaking and the dark room seemed to absorb the words which came into the ears of Jayandra faintly, as if he was being told in a dream. He kept glaring at Charan unbelievingly. At length he spoke.

"I have told you. Choose between me and Khanji."

Charan did not speak. But then he noticed the situation he was in. It was no longer one in which to keep eyes cast down. Jayandra was no longer soliciting. He stood up and seized Charan by the throat. His whole person shivered with rage.

"I'll kill you! Choose. I say, choose! Is Khanji your brother?"

Charan only shook his head, sweat oozing from his pores.

"Who is Khanji to you?"

Charan tried to move his lips. They moved slightly but he was unable to pronounce a syllable. Jayandra was mad with exasperation.

"Now why do you keep following him?" There was no answer. Then Jayandra released Charan and threw himself flat on the cold cement floor, shouting and sobbing like a child. He kept wriggling and banging against the counter with a tremendous vigour. Charan stayed there for a few seconds more, then he availed himself of the opportunity to rush through the back door and, without looking back or remembering his vehicle, he ran home.

FOURTEEN

The year 1958 was passing away. The Christmas holidays were approaching with them the end of the school year. The clouds cleared and the sun shone on Mbazala Mission. On the school quadrangle the boys had lined up before a huge crowd of onlookers. In front of them chairs were arranged in three lines. Guests from all around had been invited. They sat on these chairs and those who missed chairs crowded around the lined-up pupils. Immediately in front of the rows of chairs, three chairs were arranged behind a low table on which there were vases of hibiscus flowers. The Reverend Father Jones Waters sat in the centre with the two school teachers, Manono and Mayenge, at his sides. It was the long-awaited graduation day.

Amongst the invited guests, who were mostly the fathers from Ngaza, Mr Samuel sat. He smiled all the while and occasionally looked to the right where his eyes rested upon Chief Mathew

Gumwele, who on that day was in a black suit. The chief looked gloomy. He gazed at the ceremony, listlessly drawing on the cigarette stuck between his thin lips.

Mr Samuel looked at the chief and he recalled the little affair that had taken place in the office of the D.C. a year ago. It was when the new D.C., Mr John White, that very shrewd, cunning European, came to Bulembe. He had come to replace the old Harold Bright, who had then retired to England. Chief Gumwele came to the office of the D.C. to introduce himself. He took his wife with him and came up to the office in his land-rover. When in the office, the chief stood, his legs planted apart, and, glancing at his wife out of the corner of his eye, he said, "Sir, and here is my *memsahib*." He pointed at her. She was standing there wearing a green skirt and a white blouse. At that moment, Samuel was sorting some files on a shelf in the office. Mr White stood, his right hand in his pocket and adjusting the position of his pipe with his left, he walked briskly to the chief in two long steps.

"Pardon me, I didn't catch you," White said, chewing the words and totally terrifying the chief.

"I have brought with me my *memsahi*." . But before he finish this, Mr. White had slapped him on the right cheek, his white palm sinking in the soft flesh and leaving dents of the fingers on it.

"Do you call this monkey a *memsahib*? Who taught you that appellation?" And immediately after, with immeasurable scorn, White opened the door for Gumwele, yelling at him to leave. Since that day Mr Samuel could not help envisaging that very scene wherever he saw Chief Gumwele.

The school band came over to join the other pupils on the quadrangle. They marched gracefully, pushing away the group of parents and other onlookers who were not seated and were crowding all around the scene. The flutes gave out the high pitched tune of a familiar and popular song of the day

Brave brave King's soldiers

Came up arm in arm

Where are they, where are those?

They cried again and ever

But nobody was to dare

As this song ended, the lines were already in order. All had become quiet. The headteacher, Mr Manono, stood up to face the invited guests and made a short speech to welcome Father Waters, who was to hand out the certificates and welcome the guests. The speech was a bit hasty and Father Waters stood amidst loud cheers and clapping. The standard eight boys came up, one by one, as Mr Mayenge called out their names. They bowed very low before Waters and the guests. He gave them his skinny hand and mumbled at each of them, "With this, take the blessings of our Lord."

"Amen," said the boys shaking, as they took his hand.

It began with the prefects. The prefect of food stores, Simon Lubele, came first. The crowd clapped and cheered as he bowed low and took his school-leaving certificate. He smiled broadly, glancing at Mr Mayenge on his right.

After the prefects the name of Willie Samuel was called. He leaped forth proudly and the pupils, who took him for the incarnation of a good boy, cheered and clapped, though somewhere deep within could be felt the acutely piercing arrow of their true attitude towards him. Their faces did not brighten. Instead they took on a darker colour. The muscles tightened and the hands resisted movement. Thus the clapping ceased almost instantly and the dark faces stared at Willie as he resumed his place. Every pupil in standard eight linked his thoughts about Willie with the memory of Mangangala. Mr Samuel looked with pleasure at Willie. But he knew that there was little hope of his son's going for further studies at Ngaza seminary as he wished. Willie would never go through the exam successfully, he knew.

The handing out of certificates ended and Father Waters said a few words wishing the out-going pupils a good life, good use of the knowledge they had gained, obedience and particularly submission to the Lord Jesus Christ. The band started up again and the pupils marched out of the quadrangle. A minute or so later they came in again, one class at a time, and performed what they had prepared. Standard five came first and lastly came standard eight. These school-leavers did not perform any dances as the others did. They sang a song. That was for most of them their last song in school. It was a sad moment for all those present. This was the last moment for the school to have its same structure. Suddenly everybody realized that time was really something mobile. Tears stood in the eyes of every pupil and an invisible bond of love appeared to strain hard and resist the forces that were immediately to scatter them, a moment when everyone pardoned his enemy and the concept of hatred had no longer any meaning. The school-leavers tried hard to sing without showing much feeling but their song came out with little energy.

School life is a long journey
with its numerous ditches and thorns
But it is the price every good is bought
Good-bye Mbazala Boys', good-bye.
In that busy life of pen and paper,
it had appeared endless, boring and torturing
But today it is a pleasant nightmare
Good-bye Mbazala Boys', good-bye.

An hour later everything was over. The school compound became deserted. The boys of the lower classes had collected the desks and put them back in the classrooms. The chairs, most of which had been borrowed from Ngaza, were sent back in a mission lorry. The guests had dispersed: the fathers from Ngaza in their cars and motorcycles; chief Gumwele in his land rover driven by Kajanja, who had all the while been chatting to Meza and Magadi as they leaned against the bonnet; Mr Samuel, who, with his son, left a bit later after having some little talk with the Reverend Waters in the mission house; and the pupils with their wooden boxes on their shoulders scattering in tiny groups towards their homes.

Simon Lubele was about a mile from Mbazala Mission along the road to Bulembe when the red car passed him. It went very fast, blowing a thick cloud of dust behind it and Simon could hardly see the hand Willie waved to him from the back seat. He blinked his eyes for a while until the dust cleared. He watched the car as it rode out of his sight. It bumped up and down along the corrugated earth road. He wondered how comfortable one felt sitting in it. He had been in a vehicle before, but that was a lorry and not a car. It was when he, as the school's food prefect, had been going to fetch sacks of flour at Ngaza for their food supply. The huge thing had bumped hard and the loosely attached wooden frames of the lorry's body hustled him violently this way and that. He wondered whether Willie felt that, too, in the back seat of the beautiful little thing that had just passed him.

However, the deep feelings of leaving school did not desert him even for a brief while. He wondered how much he had thought of the school community as a permanent entity. It had seemed to be a society with a common life, common thinking and even a common end. He thought he understood it very well, each individual. But then he found this a great fallacy.

He found that he had never known anybody, that the school society had been made up of individuals with a lot of them had picked up his wooden box and disappeared without much word, each one to places known only to himself.

Simon reached Nlimanja very late that evening but his father was still at the fireside in the backyard. After taking his meal, which Nganda went back into the kitchen to make, he sat opposite his father at the fire and they talked late into the night.

"At Mpunguta I have seen a shop. Whose shop is that?" Simon enquired as he seated himself on a stool.

"It belongs to your uncle, Kamuyuga. But actually it belongs to an Indian. But Kamuyuga told me that the shop is his. I did not ask him more about this and he doesn't appear happy to discuss about his new fortune."

"Who is this Indian you say owns the shop of Uncle Kamuyuga?"

"That Indian who was murdered last year. Didn't you hear about that murder? The Indian was called Charan. Rumours say that the Indian had quarelled with other shopkeepers in the town. And it is said that these other shopkeepers are the ones who killed him. One morning his body was found just lying on that road to the mosque. So he must have been killed when coming or going to pray." Lubele was silent so abruptly that Simon thought his father's voice had dried up. Then the older man continued in a lower tone.

"And it is also said that Kamuyuga got involved in the affair. He had aligned himself with the Indians who killed Charan, so as to keep this shop as his property, which at first he was only given to take charge of."

"I heard about that death. But that Indian gave Uncle Kamuyuga a smaller shop. Was it this one? And also this one is in a new house."

"That new house you have seen is built this year and the shop has only been expanded into what you saw. It was that same little shop he had since early last year. Still he is planning to build more."

Simon sank deep in thought. He let his eyes dwell upon the flames as his thought wandered across the valley to Mpunguta.

The thought of the act of murder sent a cold shiver through him and he struggled hard to throw the thought back from whence it had come.

"Your brother, Lunja, wrote us, I received his letter last week," Lubele began again.

"Where is he living now?" Simon, hearing of this unexpected news, easily got rid of the thought of murder he had been fighting with a moment before.

"He is now living in Daisalama. In his letter he said he had written many letters to us but he never got a reply."

"But did we receive any?"

"He says he gave them to people who came to Bulembe at the bus station in Daisalama. It must have been these people who did not deliver the letters. Lunja says you should come and look for a job in Daisalama. He has sent some money also, for your fare."

"When should I go?" Simon asked, already excited.

"That will now be up to yourself. As for the fare, haven't I told you that it has come?" Simon couldn't find reason why he should sit and give any more thought. Anyday he would be ready to embark, even that same night if it had been possible.

"So I would like to go there this Monday."

"But I haven't seen your box. Didn't you bring it?"

"I felt it heavy and I was too tired. So I left it with *Shemeji* Zayumba in the town. I will go and bring it tomorrow."

It was after lunch next day when Simon walked out of his father's compound at Nlimanja, heading towards Bulembe town.

With money his father gave him, he spent some time going in and out of the shops purchasing some new clothes and a pair of rubber shoes, as preparations for his journey to Dar es Salaam.

After his humble but very careful shopping, Simon passed by the Indian-owned shop where Zayumba worked and fetched his luggage.

When he reached Mpunguta it was already sunset. He walked down the hill towards the river Mfele below. At the river valley he was greeted by the familiar noise made by the river's current, a noise he had known since birth. He walked slowly, feeling the weight of the wooden box pulling at his arm. A bucket lay on the rocks by the side of the river and a little girl sat beside it. When the bare feet of Simon thundered on the earth road the young girl screamed, giving out a sharp warning shriek.

"*Daadaa* . . . people!" Simon was urged to halt by some reflex and he stood mute, wondering. But instantly his eyes rested on a girl immersed in the stream, her head above the water level.

"Simon," she called out with the wholesome, pleasant smile of a village girl. The younger girl sitting beside the bucket had been too late to give a timely warning.

"Simon, please. . ."

"What is it, Moina?" Simon asked her, his face lighting up. He let the wooden box drop onto the path.

"Please Simon, I want to get out of the water."

"Why, does anybody hinder you? Do so."

"But at least go back a little," Moina went on imploring, with the same smile on her lips. Simon did not move.

He kept looking at her. There was apparently a curiosity he wanted to satisfy.

"Simon, please . . ." This time Simon was moved. He couldn't stand it.

"Alright, I will go." Simon went back hardly some four strides. The younger girl threw a *khanga* to her sister, who kept clinging to the river-bank rock. Moina came out and wrapped herself with it. Before she had even done so, Simon reappeared.

"Are you satisfied now?" he asked her.

"Ah! You have been peeping after all. Do you think that I did not see you?"

"No, I didn't."

"Now how did you know that I was dressed before you came again?"

"Alright; I peeped. But even if I didn't, I had seen all."

"What?"

"I say all. The water is just too clear in the first place. I saw everything," he said with triumphant amusement.

Darkness was wearing on and Moina hoisted the bucket onto her head. With her younger sister walking in front of her, Moina balanced the bucket with that skill of village women. Simon took the opposite direction and started to ascend the hill to Nlimanja, his wooden box on his left shoulder.

"So now you have come for the holidays, your work is to sit at the riverside and peep at girls bathing, isn't it?" Moina asked reproachfully, her white teeth showing in the dusk.

"Yes, it is."

"Alright. But what do you gain by doing that?"

"I gain quite a lot. You can't know how much."

Moina added something which came into the ears of Simon very faintly. He didn't bother to try to discern what she said, but bent upon his little path home.

FIFTEEN

In the latter part of the decade the land underwent great change. Some several years back a wave had started in the capital with high intensity, but it kept growing smaller and smaller as it swept far and wide across the land. For a long time Bulembe remained unstirred. But as years went by the wave gathered greater power and a time came when Bulembe, too, recorded its strength. The news broke in Bulembe one Sunday morning. From there, it was propelled all around. "A man has come from Dar es Salaam," it was said. "He speaks of expelling the white man." Nobody attempted to explain to others, and the news seemed a tail without a head.

At Mpunguta the news radiated from the shop of Kamuyuga. The shopkeeper himself had brought it home from town that same morning. All who entered the shop came out bearing it. It carried little conviction but they sent it flying from home to home.

Thus the Independence party, the Tanganyika African National Union, first found its way to Bulembe after its foundation in 1954, in Dar es Salaam. Three months later the party procured an office in Bulembe. Time played its role and TANU, from an acronym that carried little meaning to the people, crept along slowly to political organisation with defined aims. Sengene, a retired primary school teacher, resident of Mshenye, was named first chairman, Bulembe TANU Branch.

From time to time in the afternoons, public meetings were held outside the TANU office at Mshenye. The audience grew each time and with that, more and more joined TANU. People would sit there in the warm rays of the afternoon sun staring and listening to the TANU choir group that always featured at the rallies. What had before seemed unimaginable and time-wasting eventually grew into a strong, worthwhile cause.

There was a dreadful stillness over the whole town of Bulembe one afternoon. The sun shone hard but her golden rays appeared not to have much energy. This was June, the cooler season on the Anyalungu plateau. The light wind that customarily blew over the town, throwing dust upon the provisions in the market, had now calmed down. People were only occassionally to be seen going in and out of the shops. The whole town looked dead.

However, in the heavy stillness that lingered over the town centre, faint voices penetrated from the football fields that were situated down the main road past Mshenye. The whole population of the town and even some people from the villages were there, too.

There was a long table lying in front of the crowd. Lubele caught sight of Simon sitting near the choir group to the side of the table.

"Have you seen Simon?" Lubele whispered to Kamuyuga, who was sitting beside him.

"Where is he?"

"There, he is sitting beside the table, the one in the blue sweater."

"Yes, now I have seen him. Is he a member of TANU also?"

"I don't know. This is the first time I set my eyes upon him since he went to Daisalama last year. I think he has come with the other guests."

Simon had also caught sight of his father and he had guessed the subject of their discussion. At length his eyes met those of his father and he gave a short smile.

"So it is there that he has come in contact with this Independence movement," Kamuyuga concluded.

The choir group staffed singing and the crowd listened, the words drifting into their heads as if in a dream.

Watanganyika, chama chetu ni TANU

Eee wananchi, tujiunge na TANU

Mungu akipenda tupate UHURU

Mungu akipenda tupate UHURU

TANU is our party

Let's join TANU, everybody

We shall be free

If God wills

They sang various songs for twenty minutes. Then Sengene climbed onto the table and greeted the crowd with the words *Uhuru! Uhuru!* — freedom, freedom. He said a few words and then introduced someone who mounted the table and stood beside him. He was a tall fellow of about six feet and he had wrapped around himself a magnificent green *kitenge* cloth. His face brightened with a broad smile.

"Is this Nyerere?" Lubele asked his comrade, before the introduction was made.

"No, not him. I know Nyerere. He is not this man. This must be another person. Nyerere came that first time, you remember?"

"I did not attend that meeting."

"I did not attend either. Only a few people attended that first time. But I managed to see him the following day when he was going back to Daisalama."

Sengene said that that man was called Bangama, a prominent fellow in the party in Dar es Salaam. Bangama began by saying that the Party headquarters had heard of the rapid progress of TANU in Bulembe. He said the Party had therefore sent him to see how much progress there was. He said that he had greeetings for them from Julius Nyerere, whom some of them had seen when he came to Bulembe. He told the people the importance of their embracing TANU. He also said that UHURU would be near if everybody cooperated.

In the deserted streets of the town, a shiny black car drove without haste down the town along the main road. The car came blowing a little dust in its wake and at the end of the main road it turned to the right, along the road leading to the fields where the TANU meeting was taking place. As it came into sight of the crowd, all eyes turned round to see it. The attention of the crowd was for a moment given to the newcomers.

The car drove up a distance away from the scene. Its doors opened and the D.C. came out. Then Mr Samuel appeared by the other door. John White, the Bulembe District Commissioner, looked at the crowd blankly at first and then he let his eyes settle upon the person of Mr Bangama, not without much scorn.

There was an apparent uneasiness in the crowd over the presence of the white man. The people had expected Bangama to shrivel immediately after the car made its appearance. But Bangama continued without hestation.

"The fellow is really venturesome," White commented with that same scorn on his face.

"It's all foolish daring," Samuel said, shaking his head lightly and trying to show as much contempt as White.

"I will like to know personally all civil servants who indulge themselves in such things." Before White had finished saying this, his faithful and efficient clerk had already brought out a notebook from his pocket. His eyes ran through the crowd searchingly and he spotted a few of them. But he did not see Chief Gumwele, whom he thought would be there too.

The crowd kept their eyes turned towards Bangama. But the words the TANU man spoke had not so much effect as did the person of Bangama himself. Nobody listened. They only gazed at him. Everybody kept wondering how the fellow could so fearlessly speak in front of a white man, a D.C. particularly. Lubele looked at Simon constantly. His boy also made the same fearless impression. Then he noticed that all those with him had the same air about them. No fear for white men and even D.C.s. Did it mean that once someone was a TANU man then he had no fear for anything?

Lubele remembered a tale his mother told him many years ago. It was when he was still a child. She spoke of *Maji-Maji*, the great war against-Europeans. It had been assumed that anybody who took the *maji* would never be affected by the foreigners' weapons. And thus people started up the war. Unfortunately, it turned out to be a calamity. The *maji* was noprotection. Now there came into his mind this new thing, TANU, and how those in it took so much courage. Would it end up like the unfortunate *maji*? He found it a fascinating thought.

White did not stay there very long. His departure gave apparent relief to the crowd. Now they had full opportunity to concentrate upon Bangama. The confidence that he had exhibited had won him what he had not expected. When he finished speaking people queued in front of the table to buy the TANU membership cards which Bangama sold in large numbers, The TANU choir group renewed the singing and this time with much more vigour than before.

Mwingereza tupe Uhuru

Mwingereza tupe Uhuru

Tumechoka kutawaliwa

Tanganyika iwe huru

Englishman give us freedom

Englishman give us freedom

We are tired of being ruled

Tanganyika should be free

The sun was setting when the crowd dispersed. Simon came over to Lubele and Kamuyuga to greet them.

"I will be quite busy tonight," Simon told his father. "Therefore I won't be able to come home with you. I am helping the Bulembe members to organise something."

"What is that thing?" Lubele inquired anxiously.

"We are organizing a party in honour of Bangama. He has to give a good report when he goes back. So he has to see how much members are cooperating."

Simon appeared to be in a great hurry and Lubele did not have enough time to ask his son the few things he wanted to know about Lunja. Then, noticing the TANU membership card in the hands of his father, Simon inquired, "So you have already bought your card?"

"Oh, both of us have," Lubele said, admiring the little piece of paper. The young man went back to rejoin his colleagues and, led by Sengene, they headed towards the TANU office.

Kamuyuga did not go home immediately. He had been summoned by Jayandra to see him that morning. But for what reason Kamuyuga himself did not know. He hadn't gone to the Indian. Then during the long speech of Bangama that afternoon, it struck into his head the duty he had neglected. From then he felt rather restless.

"I have to pass and see *Bwana Tajiri*," he told Lubele. When Kamuyuga mentioned *Bwana Tajiri* there was nobody who asked who it was. This had to be Jayandra to whom, after the miserable death of Charan, Kamuyuga attached himself very tightly. Thus the kinsmen parted.

As usual it took quite a long time before Kamuyuga could see Jayandra. The news that Kamuyuga was waiting outside to see Jayandra had to pass so many house servants that when Jayandra appeared, Kamuyuga had already frozen with fear. Jayandra let him in by the backyard door and they proceeded to sit in the shop.

"So you have become a TANU man?"

"Why?" Kamuyuga asked, not knowing what else to say. By then Jayandra had already begun panting.

"Juma . . ." he yelled through the doorway. The summoned servant appeared, not without much alarm.

"Was he not at the meeting?" the shopkeeper asked, pointing at Kamuyuga.

"He was."

Kamuyuga felt the strength of the tension in the room. He had put himself at odds with his masters. "I apologise forgive me *Bwana Mkubwa*," he muttered.

"No, no. I had summoned you so as to warn you about these things but you didn't come so you could go to the meeting. If Khanji knows about this it can be fatal. We have warned you twice before about the same things. You are among those with Sengene, and you have bought the little green thing." Saying this Jayandra thrust his hand into the pockets of Kamuyuga and brought out the TANU membership card.

"No, we don't want TANU in Bulembe. We have let you keep the property of Charan and now you want to do what you like!"

"No, not so. I don't mean to..." Kamuyuga muttered, trying to defend himself.

"If you want to feel the strength of Khanji, then try. I will take this card and show it to him." Jayandra cut him short and, opening the door with his left hand, he pushed Kamuyuga with the right. Kamuyuga was hustled into the verandah outside and whatever he tried to say was shuttered by the banging of the huge shop doors which Jayandra sent flying behind him.

That same evening, the party in honour of Bangama took place at the Bulembe Welfare Centre. Among the invited guests were the D.C., his chief clerk, Mr Samuel, the chief and the Reverend Father Jones Waters from Mbazala Mission. The D.C. himself did not attend and he was represented by his chief clerk.

There was much cheering at the party that particular evening. The music played by the Bulembe Youngsters Jazz Band sent its waves rolling all over the town and beyond. There did not pass three minutes without mention of Nyerere, TANU or Uhuru. The excitement spread outside the hall also. The red dust of Bulembe was swept this way and that in the moonlight by cheerful youth. Whether they came to celebrate the occasion or just enjoy dancing to the music, they all took chorus with those inside.

At a table at the back of the hall, sat Mr Samuel, the` chief, Father Waters, Mr Sengene and Mr Bangama, who was the special guest at the dance that evening. They talked and drank. Mr Bangama talked most of the time while the rest only listened to him. The chief showed much interest in what Bangama talked, but not Waters or Samuel. These two seemed gloomy and uneasy. They just looked down at their full glasses of beer.

Bangama spoke of the prospects of TANU and how it had been accepted by many, other parts of the country. He spoke of the big efforts the party was making to bring *Uhuru* sooner how many other people, too, had tried to sabotage it and had failed, and so on. Sengene only kept quiet, sipping his drink from time to time. The chief appeared particularly interested to know more about the saboteurs. Bangama did not fail to narrate the various instances sabotage had been attempted and had miserably failed. In the way Bangama narrated, the whole business against TANU appeared so foolish and funny that the Anyalungu chief giggled with much amusement, glancing out of the corner of his eye at Waters, to his right. Bangama also narrated incidents where white people were involved and how they got frustrated in the end.

Father Waters couldn't bear it any longer. He felt blood rushing to his head. He whispered into the ear of Samuel, on his right.

"This is a very mannerless guest. And is Gumwele sympathizing with TANU?" the priest asked, his voice trembling with rage.

"Yes, he is one of them. I think this is because he is not on good terms with the D.C. Only that," Samuel whispered back and added, "but they will all see."

"Who?"

"Those who think themselves so clever."

"You mean TANU people?" Waters asked eagerly.

"Yes, they. The D.C. asked me to note their names. And I swear that there will be no mercy."

Waters smiled with pleasure and eyed Samuel fondly, his whole person expressing much satisfaction.

Half a minute later two people, both in the civil service —or the Queen's service, to put it in the language of those offices they worked in — came over to the table and bent over Sengene. Their faces expressed deep feelings. They took the TANU chairman two strides from the table and talked to him in whispers. They spoke very solicitously bending their necks this way and that. The face of Sengene changed from that of brightness to that of solemnity. He listened to them thoughtfully as they talked, his eyes cast down. Then he took them back to the table.

"Excuse me, gentlemen," he began, interrupting the narrative about the saboteurs. The solemn face of Sengene alarmed the rest. They turned their attention and looked up to the intruders. Sengene went on.

"These two gentlemen have a favour to ask from one among our guests tonight. It is from Mr Samuel. They have come to learn that their names have been recorded at the meeting when his honour, the D.C., came."

Bangama had not the least idea as to who took down the names. "What!" he exclaimed, his manly expressing much ridicule over the deed. The chief also thought it to have been the D.C. himself and he did not hesitate to look down upon the action.

"Do we have saboteurs in this place, also?" Bangama said, looking around appealingly at Waters and Samuel, both of whom never even looked up. Gumwele took it up.

"Yes, the same type of saboteurs in Bulembe, as well as in Dar es Salaam and elsewhere, you have just related," he said, even finding the whole event more amusing. "The devils are here also!" he added.

There was no more patience in the chief clerk or the priest. They stood up one after the other.

"No, no!" Samuel shouted, his eyes already red with blood. He wanted to fling the glass he had in his hand at one of his enemies, as he thought them to be, but Sengene grabbed it from him.

"No, no, no — this won't be!" he said, hardly pronouncing the words. But then those who were dancing, away from the table, had noticed the trouble. They soon surrounded the little group. Waters grabbed the arm of the chief clerk and led him out of the hall to where their cars were parked. The crowd followed them to the door and watched them as they started their cars and drove away at high speed, one behind the other.

SIXTEEN

The independence movement for most people of Bulembe was much beyond their understanding, despite the many meetings that were organized from time to time. However, the people showed much interest in the affairs of the party. Whether *Uhuru* would materialize as they heard in the speeches by party officials or not, to them the Party was still very enterprising. It had become apparent that TANU was an organ preoccupied with the fate of their subjugators, the colonialists. The boldness of party leaders in teasing the white race became a fascinating spectacle. Everybody enjoyed it and TANU membership rose in huge numbers.

Kamuyuga, since the time Bangama came to Bulembe, had ceased to be a TANU member. The quarrel with his Indian allies had turned him into an active enemy of TANU. On that same night he had gone straight across Mfele to Nlimanja. Lubele had hardly been a half hour in bed when Kamuyuga knocked. Lubele opened the door for him. Alarm was apparent on his face. The night visit had not been expected. They sat at the hearth in the dim light of the oil lamp Nganda brought out to them.

The night visitor did not want to beat about the bush. He had known Lubele long enough and well enough and the way to deal with him was not through trial and error. Kamuyuga told Lubele that they had done a great wrong to buy the TANU membership cards and even to have attended the meeting, that TANU was a dangerous organisation which would straight away lead to misery. He did not forget to tell him the opinions of Jayandra and Khanji.

Lubele had not said much. He was the one less informed about the whole affair, as he thought himself.

"I didn't know all this," he replied. Kamuyuga, who had been anxious to hear what Lubele would say, then looked half-satisfied. But he still had something held in his heart, which he did not want to release immediately. Then after five minutes of talking over some other matters, he began.

"Did Simon say he would come tomorrow?"

"Yes."

Kamuyuga then kept back as if fighting with something within himself. Then he forced the words out.

"Warn your son about this new thing, TANU," he spoke, looking down upon the dying embers. Lubele did not show signs of agreement or denial and Kamuyuga discerned doubt hanging about his kinsman.

"Or do you find it difficult to give advice to your own son because he has been to Daisalama?"

"No, not so." Lubele answered sharply, fearing what was to be concluded about his situation.

"I will also come tomorrow when Simon arrives, so that I can give help in the matter," Kamuyuga added as he left.

Simon came to Nlimanja the following afternoon. His visit had not been long. Soon after his arrival Kamuyuga made his appearance. After only a short time Lubele fell upon the son. The face of Kamuyuga kept haunting him, forcing his patience out. But the matter came out very differently from what the old fellows had expected. It appeared that Lubele was only interested in getting off the heavy load that he then found pressing, more than he could bear. He did not go round the bush but straightaway introduced the wishes of Jayandra and Khanji.

"But why do you go about looking for the opinions of Indians, Father?" Simon questioned. He had no knowledge that the mastermind behind his father was the bush shopkeeper sitting with mounting hysteria just opposite him.

"Who are Khanji or Jayandra to the people of Bulembe or even to you?" Simon went on and on, despising the idea and its authors without the least caution.

Lubele, feeling that he had fullfiled what was wanted of him by Kamuyuga, never bothered himself with much arguing. He kept quiet and looked satisfied. He felt himself a freed man. He began talking of new topics and did not notice what was going on in Kamuyuga. And Kamuyuga, seeing something he had felt to be important treated in this manner, took his leave and went away.

After that short talk over the party, Lubele became assured of safety in his membership. He took the TANU card off the stool where it lay and treasured it in his wooden box.

Five days passed. Simon had gone back to Dar es Salaam. In the afternoon Nganda sat in her little kitchen at Nlimanja, after her *shamba* work. For a long time she sat on the low stool, staring at the boiling pot on the tiny hearth in front of her. It was already past lunch time, she thought. Lubele would be coming back from the *shamba* where she had left him. Then without giving much thought to it she swung round and reached for a bottle in which she kept her rock salt crystals. She lifted it to pour out some in her palm. Five small crystals came out and no more. There was no salt in the house.

At that moment, Lubele appeared. He walked into the backyard slowly and hustled his hoe to a corner. Nganda had not noticed him until he came and stood in the kitchen doorway.

"Is the meal not ready? What have you been doing all this time?" his voice was weak with hunger and hard work. Nganda stood up and went into the living house. She picked up two ten-cent coins and, fetching the empty bottle in the kitchen, walked out of the compound along the path to Mpunguta. Her short legs worked fast and she was soon carried across the valley.

At Mpunguta, Kamuyuga sat in his shop after lunch. There had been no customer for a whole hour and he began feeling sleepy. When he noticed Nganda walking towards the shop he bent down his head and let it drop on his arms which were folded on the counter. Nganda drew up in front of the counter."

"*Shikamoo, shemeji,*" she greeted him. Kamuyuga kept quiet. Nganda ignored it. Her eyes ran along the shelves in the shop until they rested upon the crystals of rocksalt that were heaped to the right of Kamuyuga.

"I greet you, *bwana*. Are you sick?" She repeated after a while, "Give us table salt. Your brother hasn't eaten anything up till now. We have had no salt" she continued, as she let the coins drop onto the counter.

Kamuyuga still did not rise.

"There is no salt here," he murmered at last, with little audibility. Nganda did not understand.

"Give us salt, *shemeji,*" she repeated. "No salt, you say?"

"I have told you that there is no salt here. Why, are you deaf?" he replied, raising his voice all of a sudden. There was something in the voice of Kamuyuga that recorded in a special place in the head of Nganda. She looked puzzled. She wondered if they misunderstand each other. But another thought came into her mind and she suddenly rushed out of the shop and walked back.

Lubele took the incident very lightly at first. Whether he believed what Nganda told him or not, it was soon realized that the necessity of salt at the time was still there. Taking the coins from Nganda, he collected himself and walked slowly down the hill and came up again at Mpunguta. Kamuyuga was still in the shop but this time he sat upright. Lubele went straight to the counter. Anybody who came close to where Lubele then stood could see the heap of rocksalt before him at first glance. Lubele saw it, too.

Kamuyuga had expected the visit somehow. He didn't look Lubele in the face. Lubele greeted him. The shopkeeper replied in a low, weak voice, not looking up.

"What has happened to Nganda! She says that you told her that there was no salt here. What is that pile in the boxes?" Lubele spoke without any notable emotion. He aimed at chastising his wife, whom he thought had misunderstood and conveyed false information just to create discord.

But Kamuyuga took it up too hastily. He never even stopped to consider what Lubele had meant to say. It was apparent that he had prepared himself for the occasion.

"This is my own shop," he began so loudly that anyone out of the compound would still hear. He now looked straight into the face of Lubele. "I can sell or not sell, whatever I want I can do." Lubele, having not expected it, just stood there amazed. But Kamuyuga continued. "You agreed with your son that I am nothing but a stooge, a lackey of Jayandra and Khanji. You said also that it is stupidity to take the opinion of Indians. Now go and buy salt from those not lackeys. From this day you shouldn't buy your needs from this shop because I am a stooge of Indians. Go and look for your needs in the TANU office. That's all."

After saying this Kamuyuga went out of the shop leaving the landlord Lubele where he stood.

SEVENTEEN

Two years later, *Uhuru*, the dreamed Independence, materialized. On the 9th of December 1961, the *Uhuru* day, the celebrations in Bulembe came. Nobody could in anyway compare the celebrations of *Uhuru* with any others before: beer parties, demonstrations, football matches, choirs dancing and many other events so that everybody was enjoying himself actively in one way or another.

However, like any other giant miracle, *Uhuru* did not seem true to many. But since *Uhuru* was commonly taken to mean the departure of white rule, the term took on more credibility when eventually the colonialist administrators evacuated.

People reasoned the unparalled celebrations couldn't just be an effect without cause. There were no people who failed to cherish the uprooting of masters so towering as the colonialists had been. It appeared not to be necessary to think deeply of life in the future, for the prospects opened up themselves clearly, even in the heads of children. That would have been like a leper sitting down to think deeply about how he felt one day after getting rid of leprosy.

Two years after *Uhuru*, in 1963, Simon came to stay in Bulembe as TANU district secretary. He found the town changing fast, as fast as any other town he had seen after *Uhuru*. There were many more businesses opening up here and there. There were a lot of new things written on doors — African bazaars, African stores, African bakeries and so many enterprises started up by Africans, some flourishing and others nearly collapsing within only a year or so after their establishment.

The TANU district office was transferred to Majengo and Simon rented a house at Majengo, just next door. In the office he had many visitors. Some visitors only came to greet him or Mr Sengene, who was still the Bulembe TANU chairman. But more often they came to lodge complaints about the Indian and African businessmen who employed them, or about some favouritism in a government office, and so on.

Simon had just got seated in his office one morning when a new, long, French-made car hooted its brakes outside the office. Simon looked up.

"Hallo, Simon," somebody called, getting out of the car. Simon recognized him. He ran out to meet the visitor.

"Hallo, Willie, where did you hide yourself all this long time?" he said, taking the hand of his old friend at Mbazala Boys' School.

"I had gone to England. By the way, I think you know that Father Waters went back to England immediately after *Uhuru?*"

"I think I heard about it."

"So, he took me with him. But when I reached there, I could not get a place for my studies because of my asthma and that is why I'm now here."

"Why, let's sit in the office." By that time two people had entered the office, unnoticed by Simon, and had seated themselves on a bench that lay beside the table. They were Lubele and Saidi-wa-Manamba. Simon began the introduction.

"Willie, here is my father, Mzee Lubele Ndanganga, and here is Mzee Saidi. He is known throughout the town. I hope that you may have known him also."

"No, I don't know him," Willie returned, shaking his head.

"You don't know him, truly?"

"No, I think I may have never known him," Willie stressed.

"And this is the son of Mr Samuel," Simon went on, looking at the old people and touching Willie on the shoulder. As for the introduction of Willie, it had sufficed to mention Samuel.

Willie found the introduction not worthwhile enough to interrupt their conversation. He went on. "You asked me where I will be living now?"

"Oh, yes."

Willie looked down. Then he raised his head slowly and his eyes beamed with satisfaction and pride. Simon noted that Willie had grown very big. But he had little changed from the naughty boy of Mbazala School.

"My father is holding one of the highest posts in the government. I hope that this you know."

"Not exactly. I only know that he is having some post in Dar es Salaam," Simon answered after a moment's failure to recollect any further knowledge about Mr Samuel.

"A principal secretary."

"So are you to stay with him in Dar es Salaam?"

"I can stay anywhere. My father has bought the big farm of that European, Mr Brown of Ngaza. You remember the oranges we used to get from him at Mbazala?"

Before Willie had finished saying this, Saidi-wa-Manamba joined him. He exclaimed, "Very true! Even the whole population of Ngaza can find labour in the farms of Samuel. Men in the pyrethrum farm; women in the rice and banana farms. Others also in the poultry farm. Eee .. !" Saidi exclaimed.

"Not only that," Willie came up, with many gestures. "What of the cattle and goats? What of the wheat farm and the big shop under the charge of my uncle?"

"Yes, yes. In the whole of Ngaza that is now the biggest shop. I say your father has really brought a blessing to the people of Ngaza. Because now they don't have to come to Bulembe," Saidi finished, looking around at the faces that attended his narration to see if there was anything else he needed to add. Then he found it at last. "This is the product of *Uhuru*. Now it is the turn of the black man."

A short silence prevailed and everyone looked down. It looked as if each was thinking about his own things. But they were all thinking of one thing. The two older people thought even more deeply. This Samuel. Was he a human being? Always climbing higher and higher. But he must be a human being, just as were the other bigger ones they had seen. People like John White and others in Bulembe and elsewhere, presiding over much wealth and power, with highly esteemed names. But White was a white man. Others like Khanji were Indians. There was not much they knew about them. They never knew how these people lived before they came to Bulembe. The first day the people of Bulembe knew them, they were clinging to what they had then. Khanji had his shops and lorries. The white one, also. He had maintained his feared position with the same firm grip.

Lubele then recalled a story narrated by his son-in-law, Zayumba, one evening many years ago at Nlimanja. The fire round which they had sat gave a steady radiation that penetrated softly, making the old man feel sleepy. He had lain back in the easy chair and the conversation among the young people came to him only faintly. Zayumba, who sat opposite Lubele, had begun.

"The first Indian I worked for had a very fat wife. She was very strict but she was at times very moody. One day, she sent me to buy meat at the market and when I brought it back, the change I was given by the butcher was not correct. I had been given less money. At that time I didn't know how to count money, you know. So the fat Indian woman kept shouting at me that whole morning. And I hadn't any money so as to repair the wrong that I had done, so I said nothing. After lunch she began again and when I found it not going to end I decided to tell her I hadn't handled money before. So she stopped after a little while but she told me to pay the missing money when I got my salary at the end of the month.

"Three days later she began again, but her mood was not so bad that day. We were sitting behind the shop that evening. Her husband had gone to pray and the shop had been closed. 'Zayumba,' she called me, her voice a bit tender that day. 'You don't know how to count coins, but it is not your fault, poor you! You know, long in the past, God created three people' she said, looking at me and showing three fingers on her left hand"

Till then the words had been entering the ears of Lubele very softly. When Zayumba reached this point the old one, who was about to doze off, had shaken off sleep and his eyelids parted. He listened. Zayumba had gone on quoting the Indian woman.

"The three people were a European, an Indian and an African. Then God asked each of them in turn. He said, 'What do you want to have on earth? Then, the European said, 'I want wisdom and power.' God gave him. Next came the turn of the Indian. He said to God, 'I want shops and coins.' And God gave him. When the turn of the African came, he asked God saying, 'I want drums and women!'"

All this passed in a single flash in the mind of Lubele as he sat in the Bulembe TANU office. Then his cogitations returned to Samuel. He lifted his head and let his eyes search Willie. He remembered him as a small child when he had gone one day to their house with a present of bananas some years back. Willie had never in his life dressed like any other child of Bulembe. His father was in most aspects even more different. But why so strange? he thought. These were not among the less-known ones — White or Khanji. These were the Anyalungu of Ngaza, true sons of Njunju. Their present position must have been purely artificial, he concluded.

"Do you know anything about Carolina?" Willie asked Simon, breaking the heavy silence.

"You mean the chief's daughter?"

"Yes, the eldest daughter who has Dar es Salaam?"

"By the way, what is the chief himself doing in Dar es Salaam?"

"I can't say exactly. When I left for England I saw him in Dar es Salaam. He was then trying to make up a business. And when I came back I didn't ask. But I have a feeling that besides his business he is also in the government service."

"So what about her?" Simon asked, lowering his tone. Willie looked reproachfully at him. His eyes searched the eyes of Simon as if looking for some hidden information. Then he opened his lips and gave out mere whispers.

"She has completed her standard twelve and teacher education. I am going to marry her two months hence." After this Willie's mood changed. He pretended to bury himself deep in thought and played with his fingers. He started again after a time. "England ..." he said, as if addressing himself. "If it weren't for the fools! I would not have been here now."

"Which fools?" Simon wondered.

"Ah! Those who kept rejecting me because of my asthma." The older fellows appeared bored by the latter part of the young men's conversation. They soon broke into their own.

"Is Bwana Alkarim well?" Saidi-wa-Manamba asked Lubele.

"Who is this?"

"You don't know who Alkarim is? That brother of yours who owns a shop at Mpunguta. Is he not now called Alkarim?"

These words made Lubele feel totally displaced.

"Why?" he asked, without having thought of the question.

Saidi turned to him, his eyes searching the inner side of Lubele. How could it be? he wondered. Then he spoke. "You ask why, do you not know that your brother is turning Muslim? He came to my house one day and asked me how I felt in being a Muslim. I told him that I felt quite all right and he said that he had been admiring me all the time since his arrival from Pwani. He said that he had wanted to become a Muslim since that time he lived in Pwani. But he didn't do so. So now his time has come."

"What is his new name you just mentioned — Alkam ... ?" Lubele stumbled over the new syllables.

"Alkarim, Alkarim, not Alkam," Saidi stressed, laughing at him. It had appeared so funny to him that for the next two minutes

Saidi-wa-Manamba went on laughing, shedding tears on his white *kanzu*. After a time he recovered.

"All his family is going to take up new Muslim names," Saidi went on. "He told me that names like Mashaka make a bad impression and they foretell a bad future for the person. And those like Kamuyuga, Mugindi and many other Anyalungu names are not human. They belong to the devils of long ago. A time even long before Njunju."

Finishing this, Saidi-wa-Manamba put on an air of business. He sat up on the bench and interrupted the talk that had been going on simultaneously between Simon and Willie.

"Can I hope to see the chairman?" he said, addressing the TANU secretary.

"Who, Mr Sengene?"

"Yes, it is him I came to see."

"I am sorry to tell you that Sengene has resigned, though not officially. He was here last week but I heard that he had come to fetch his belongings and his family."

"Resigned, who? Our TANU chairman?" Lubele asked.

Before Simon could answer, Willie took it over. He said, "Sengene, that tall chap? I saw him in Dar es Salaam at the house of Chief Gumwele one day. He told the chief that he had worked hard for Uhuru, which has now been achieved. And now it is his time to see whether the *uhuru* he had been fighting for so hard is of some value or not. So he has started up a business at Morogoro. I think I heard something like that."

"I also heard of this business at Morogoro." Simon said, nodding. Then turning to Saidi, he asked, "Was it so necessary that you see him?"

"Ah, don't worry. It was nothing of importance."

"And where is that Bangama?" Lubele asked eagerly. Saidi did not fail to beg the question, as was his habit.

"Yeees — that tall Bangama, I still remember him. We don't hear of him!"

"He also resigned, didn't you know? He is now only a member, an ordinary one like you."

"Why did he resign?" Saidi pressed.

"People are now busy with money. He is now running a transport company; I don't know exactly where. But I know that he is no longer a TANU leader."

After this the office fell quiet again. The eyes of Saidi-wa-Manamba ran from left to right for a time and something popped up in his head. There was something heavy pulling down at his heart all the time the conversations had been going on. He had wanted to clear it but his lips hadn't moved to speak. It was about the introduction that had been made. He had not been satisfied with it. He cleared his throat and began.

"*Baba,* you say you don't know Saidi-wa-Manamba of Mshenye? I used to come to your house many times and on several times your father sent me to Ngaza. One time in 1956, your mother was ill and your father sent me to look for a witchdoctor. I went to a certain doctor I knew and brought him to your house. The doctor used to lodge at Mkomolo but now he is dead. And at the time the doctor was at your home, I came everyday."

By the time Saidi finished this, Willie was already sweating with shame. He found this new claim to dishonour his family beyond his endurance.

"No, no, no! That can't be!" he cried, his eyes already dyed red. He stood up and bent upon Saidi. He shouted so vehemently that tiny drops of saliva from his mouth spewed onto the face of the legendary *manamba* officer.

"It can't be," Willie yelled. "My father, a good, Christian student of Ngaza seminary and pupil of Father Waters, wouldn't have indulged in the scum of the heathens!" The last words came when the son of Samuel was already out of the office. He strode to his car and immediately drove off, his car's exhaust pipe sending dust particles dancing in the doorway.

EIGHTEEN

Several more years after *Uhuru* had gone by. Mpunguta and Bulembe had changed greatly. There were many more people in the town itself and with the increase, more buildings had been erected. The clusters of mud houses roofed with thatch had been largely replaced by brick buildings with glimmering corrugated iron sheets on top of them. And this time these were arranged in proper streets. The very numerous business installations which erupted in the early aftermath of *Uhuru* were by then reduced to only a few. It looked as if some of the businessmen had been giving as good as they got to their rivals. For the differences between them kept growing so rapidly that many soon found themselves at the feet of their rivals asking to be employed, just like those they themselves had employed in better times.

Mpunguta had grown relatively bigger. There were many more houses and things, too. If you took the route from Bulembe to

Mpunguta you would read on a big signboard just before reaching where Kamuyuga used to live, printed in huge capitals, HAMNIWEZI STORE and below this, in smaller writing, ALKARIM & SONS. If you had known persons by the names of Kamuyuga, Mugindi, and Mashaka, then you would have to change to Alkarim, Amina and Juma respectively. As a courtesy you couldn't call somebody by an old, rejected name and here you would have to get used to the changes.

At Hamniwezi, as people of Mpunguta and all around used to call the residence of Alkarim, there was a permanent atmosphere of liveliness. There was no time during

the day when there were not people playing *bao* in the verandah of the shop. This had become the centre of Mpunguta.

For the people of Mpunguta, Hamniwezi became their town. When they felt bored or lonely at home and wished to find themselves something interesting, they would drag themselves over to sit on the verandah at Hamniwezi, watching the many people who came to shop or just visiting, or merely watching those who played *bao*. If it was nighttime then it was enough to sit and fix ones eyes at the brightly shining petromax and watch the beetles that swarmed, cheering the bright light. When Alkarim himself was not there the team of servants would chatter loudly, making a lot of noise, and yell at girls, calling them every name that happened to come into their minds.

At night the place slept dead except for Kadufi, who was the night watchman strolling around the buildings. He would pace along the verandahs to the poultry house which stood some twenty metres adjacent to the main house. He would not do this for very long. When midnight came he would find himself a dark place, where he would lean against some box or other, wrap himself in the heavy sheets and blankets which during his stroll were slung over his left shoulder, and thus would sleep soundly.

Saturday was the day when Zaleme came from Bulembe in his pick-up with cow meat for the Hamniwezi butchery. The other days he sold meat at Hamniwezi butchery in the Bulembe market square.

The backyard was nonetheless filled with life. There were the wives of Zaleme, Juma and their children; there was Amina herself, there were two girls who had come to live with the Alkarims from relatives at Mkomolo, but these were by then no less than paid house servants. These were not the only people to be seen in the backyard. There was Zayumba sitting beside the oven baking bread or *chapatis,* making tea or doing the landlady's housework. Juma was the dealer in the shop. He used to sit on the verandah playing *bao* until somebody came to buy one thing or another. Juma would still continue playing bao while the customers kept standing at the counter. He would do so until a time came when he jerked himself at leisure and went to serve the already - indignant customers. Like the Indian shopkeepers who were his model, he knew it would never do to serve customer with rapidity and courtesy. Then they did not respect you.

Alkarim himself had no particular assignment. He would often be seen standing on the door steps outside the shop, dressed in a *shuka* tucked in at the waist. His belly, which had grown very big during the past seven years of success, took cover under a green cotton shirt which he never took off regularly for washing or even just a change. He would stand there most of the time, looking and shouting at the different people who came into his sight. Saidi-wa-manamba had become part of the place by visiting Hamniwezi every other day. He would lounge on the verandahs and try to get the attention of Alkarim or other members of the house by commenting on this and that. He would finally be offered a cup of tea by some member of the household and after that he would continue lounging on the verandahs or playing *bao*.

On one afternoon the landlady was seated on a finely woven mat that was sprawled on the cement floor inside one of her rooms. It was a sunny afternoon and the corrugated iron roof harboured a lot of heat, which made her feel very sleepy. She had sat there for more than two hours, her legs stretched on the mat and leaning against the wall. She listened without much interest to the chatting that went on in the backyard. Her eyes were fixed at the clean, smooth, bare feet she laid on the mat, but her thoughts were wandering very far away. She remembered the words her husband had told her one day long ago. That was long before *Uhuru*.

Alkarim had told her about the life he was going to find her. He told her that in the future she would have servants to till her *shambas*, do her housework, wash her clothing and that she would sit on a mat, her legs stretched out and her hands busy knitting, just as the Bulembe Indian women did.

Now she realised that that time had come. The whole story had become a reality. She felt remorse at having thought ill of her husband when their earlier, tiny business had collapsed. Now she felt that Alkarim was everything for her. He was the only worthwhile husband. She felt that she loved him more than ever before. He was a good man. There

was only one problem — suddenly he seemed eager to take another wife, one who was yet a young girl. But that did not completely cancel out the high position her husband held in her life.

Her thoughts went again to those times which now came back into her head only once a year or so. She remembered that little business which had made her neglect her rice fields and pay money to Andunje to till the maize fields. And that five shillings she owed Andunje had remained a harassing debt for quite a while, and Andunje never gave her time to breathe. He had gripped tight. But now the same Andunje was tilling the whole valley of the river Mfele for her year after year. And there was no day when he harassed her for pay or what. It was only when she fancied and took pity on him that she threw something or other at him and he just smiled. There were the servants who did all her housework plus that of her daughters-in-law. She was there, sitting, her legs stretched out, with everything exactly as Alkarim had foretold. She thought that this was no case of foretelling the future, but rather that he had promised her and made good his promise. Now only one thing was lacking. She didn't know how to knit. She was sitting here, but not exactly like the Bulembe women. Her fingers did not know how to twist the threads. But she could teach herself and one day it would be complete.

For a brief moment her thoughts flew back to the period in the eight years her husband had been at Pwani, a time when she carried bananas on that very head to Bulembe to find money to buy herself the *kanikis* she wore. A cold shiver ran down her whole spine and the sleepiness shook off her. No, that was not her life. She had been living, yes, she admitted. But that must have been something intermediary to "life". These thoughts faded slowly and her mind returned to where she was sitting. She remembered that the next day was the Idd-el-Haji day and Alkarim had told her that there would be a lot of guests.

"Zayumba!" she called. Zayumba, who had been very busy at the oven baking special bread and *samosas* for the next day, did not hear. Amina called again, a bit louder. This time Zayumba heard and dashed into the house.

"When you are called why don't you respond or come immediately? Do you think that I have the voice to keep shouting out names unnecessarily?"

"Ah, I didn't hear, mama."

"What!" The wife of Juma yelled, coming into the room. "Does he say that he didn't hear? Why, the voice came out quite audibly," she stressed, gesticulating wildly.

"I know that he heard," the landlady agreed with her daughter-in-law.

"This Zayumba is very stubborn nowadays, Mama. If you tell him to do something you find that he takes a long time before doing it," she added, going out of the house.

"Go and fetch water. I want to have a warm bath just now."

Zayumba took a bucket and ran down the hill to the river. Not more than four minutes later he panted up the hill back into the compound. He warmed the water and sent it to the bathroom.

Amina took a long time to wash, looking at herself in the mirror all the while. She finished washing herself and then came the smearing of ointments on the face. She did it very delicately as if it were on the face of a baby. When she came out she walked briskly and passed by the hot, smoky room where Zayumba was working. "See to it that everything is clean today, because tomorrow there will be a lot of people coming." Zayumba turned his face to her, his eyes red and full of tears from the smoke that filled the little room. Amina did not wait for anything more. She went straight to bed.

On that same afternoon, Simon Lubele had decided to visit Nlimanja. He had just come home after his office work and walked slowly, swinging the torch he carried in his right hand. For a long distance he walked without thinking of anything in particular. Then his hand slipped into his pocket and he got the feel of some papers. It was a letter he had received the day before from his brother Lunja. From then on his head was filled with the thoughts of the correspondence exchanged between him and his brother.

He continued walking and thinking thus until he reached the outskirts of Mpunguta. He halted and gazed at the houses that stood before him in clusters bigger than those he used to see in his school days. The village

had really grown larger, he thought. This had been the case particularly since Independence. He had seen new houses being built all the times he went to Nlimanja but he did not bother to notice the change in growth. Slowly he started walking on again. He came to the signboard which he saw everyday that he passed there. Still he read it for the hundredth time. ALKARIM & SONS — HAMNIWEZI STORE.

Soon he was past the Hamniwezi Store and he began to descend the hill to the river Mfele. His eyes wandered everywhere within sight. At last he stood on the rocks at the river. For a long time he stood on the bare granite looking down at the clear water as it flowed past. He thought that the current was not water. It was rather a film that had recorded a life, a whole life. He could see a long story on the film. It went backwards on and on, uncoiling until it reached that day when he ran into Moina bathing at the same spot wheile he now stood. He found himself laughing very loudly as he ran up the hill to Nlimanja.

At Nlimanja, Simon sat for a long time talking to the old man. Lubele had not said much at the beginning but when it neared the time when Simon was about to leave, Lubele, came up suddenly and talked at length about his relations with the man now called Alkarim. He never called him by that new name. He either called him Kamuyuga or just referred to him as "this man".

"He says that I envy him and that I have been attempting witchcraft over his family. In the first few years after our quarrel all people took sides with me. But the riches eventually bought all of them. Look at your brother-in-law, Zayumba, for instance. Now he is so ashamed that he can't even stand before me. He is enslaved by money. And people say that he is not even given any money. Only that his wife, your sister, collects meat from the butcher. In fact all people who go to him and claim to be dear to him get nothing. Instead they continue building up his wealth and status and keep wearing off their own resources. Your sister doesn't visit us. Shame has covered her."

Simon listened patiently and let the old fellow finish what he had to say, as he wished. He found the narrative difficult to interrupt, and chose to wait for the arrival of his brother Lunja, whom he expected to come back soon.

"Do you say that your brother is still living in Daisalama?" Lubele spoke, after leaving aside his affairs with Alkarim.

"Yes, he is still there and as I have just read to you in the letter, he proposes to come next month, and if possible he will take Moina with him when he goes back." Lubele was left without words. Somewhere in his heart he thought that he didn't see success in this proposed marriage. But there was nothing that he said about it.

On his way back to Majengo, Simon spotted a figure in bright blue *khangas*. *As* he neared her he found that it was a girl, and at last he recognised her as Moina. Moina came close and Simon reversed his direction. They walked very slowly; Moina in front. As they approached Mpunguta it was already getting dark. They halted.

Moina talked little but kept nodding or lightly shaking her head when she meant a negative thing. That was nothing awkward. It was typical of their society and Simon felt that he liked it very much. Other people, girls and boys, passed them and whispered things in each other's ears. Simon and Moina looked at them long whenever they were not watched.

"He has written me a letter and I got it yesterday. He says that he will come next month." Simon said the words faintly, tickling her eardrums pleasantly. He waited for a reply from Moina but she only drew lines on the loose soil with her big toe. Simon continued. "So when he comes you will be able to fix the engagement then."

Moina beamed and gradually failed to hide her pleasure. She smiled broadly. "I am going," she said and without waiting for anything more she ran and disappeared.

NINETEEN

The next day at ten in the morning there was already a big crowd at Hamniwezi. Alkarim had alighted from his pick-up van with a lot of people dressed in white *kanzus* and caps. Some had coats on top of their *kanzus*. There were Saidi-wa-manamba and other town Muslims. They were all very happy. The Idd-el-Haji prayers had gone by a half hour before and now their remained the long-awaited celebrations.

A lot of people from Mpunguta came there, too, even Kadufi, who, accomplishing the night watch when the compound of the Alkarims awoke, had gone home and changed the heavy sheets and blankets and by then had come back in feasting gown. The guests seated themselves on the many mats that were already laid down since early morning. The *bao* board was brought out of the house and they started playing. Saidi-wa-manamba played very skillfully, scoring most points. He defeated most of those who were there. The crowd cheered at him, every one finding enjoyment in the game.

At length the giant trays containing *biriani* were laid on the mats here and there. The *bao* was deserted and the crowd now found more delight in the trays. They fell upon them. It became quiet for a time and everybody listened to the fine job his teeth could do. Alkarim himself did not eat. He called for an easy –chair and seated himself on the verandah, facing the feasting guests.

"Alli...." He called one of the house boys. Alli appeared. "Bring me water to drink." Alli brought the water in a glass.

"Which water is this?"

"Water from Mfele."

"No, bring me that rain-water: I want water that comes, from Allah." He gave back the glass to Alli. Allii reappeared after a while with the desired rain-water, which Alkarim gulped down to the last drop.

"Bwana Alkarim," Saidi-wa-manamba called. "How about you? Come and we eat together?

"Ah, you just keep on. Don't worry about me," Alkarim replied.

"Oh, that is the way Alikarim is," Kadufi chimed in as he paused for the biriani to go down his gullet. "He always cares for others first. He doesn't want things to go his way first. Look! Here is the whole of Mpunguta, relatives or no relatives. Once they know that this is a holiday, they keep pouring in here. I can even see people of Mkomolo here," Kadufi said, pointing beyond the hills and gazing hard at Mbembela, the only person who had come from Mkomolo. Mbembela kept bending over the tray of *biriani*, sending down lump after lump, as if unaffected by the comments from Kadufi.

Alkarim, now sitting up in his easy-chair, began.

"Ah, now where people say Bwana Alkarim is rich, Alkarim is rich, what do you think? You know, Bwana Saidi, if an African is rich it is very different from an Indian who can have the same amount of wealth. If an Indian is rich then he will keep locking his money in the bank. However poor you can be, begging him day after day, he won't even look at you. I can tell you, Bwana Saidi, that up to this day there is no African who has co-operated successfully and become at true friend of an Indian, or who even knows their language.

"But for us Africans, when they say, Alkarim is rich, it doesn't mean me. Why? Do I eat double what others do? Or do I sleep filling more than one bed? I say yes, I am rich. But I know that it is not me who makes use of the riches."

"Oh, this everybody knows," Kadufi came in again. "He doesn't even have the time to use his riches. Everyday people come here 'we ask a lift to Bulembe', or this and that.

He gives them. People come here day after day to borrow money without even feeling shame. Those who feel shame send their wives. On the part of the women too, they take from him sugar, meat, anything. Bwana Saidi, I say this Bwana Alkarim is still doing good things. I would now say that his kindness has exceeded the limit."

"In truth," Saidi-wa-Manamba took up, "this *baba*, Alkarim, is the only worthwhile person in all these areas. I would even say in the whole of Bulembe," he finished, pushing in his mouth a lump of biriani.

"You know," Alkarim began again, "this *Uhuru* has brought a lot of new ideas. Because the *Uhuru* says that it is time we Africans find the value we did not know that we had in ourselves. Formerly we thought that Europeans and Indians are superior. But this is not true. I have told this to Zayumba," Alkarim swung round in his easy-chair and pointed at Zayumba, who was standing there serving the feasting guests. "I said to him, 'You, Zayumba, for how long will you continue to work for Indians? This is now *Uhuru*. Come and work for Africans, too, because now we are independent and we have got our country in our hands. Now, we Africans are the bosses'. So now Zayumba, on thinking hard about this, decided to come and work for me, as you see him here."

Zayumba smiled broadly and, believing this to be a great reward acknowledging his services, he pretended not to have heard or taken it into consideration. He made himself very busy running to and from the kitchen, clanging trays against the piles of *bakulis*.

They finished eating and washed their hands. They didn't resume the *bao* immediately, but spread out on the mats and continued talking.

"Now Bwana Saidi, imagine how this Bwana Alkarim got all these riches," Kadufi said.

"I know, I know," Saidi murmured, trying his best to evade the eyes of Alkarim.

"He carried bananas on his head and sat at the market place, selling. And I can assure you, Bwana Saidi, that this Alkarim knows how to save money very well, although nowadays he looks a bit extravagant. Look at Lubele. Theystarted selling bananas almost at the same time. They sat there side-by-side. But what does Lubele have now? Nothing!"

"Ah, that's true," Saidi said coldly. "He has nothing. And I can't know how it all happened."

"Oh, it is this, you know," Kadufi continued. "You know between them there was a great difference. This Baba Alkarim is a travelled man. He has seen many things at Pwani and elsewhere. So when he came back he had a lot of plans. Now the case of this friend of mine is quite different. When he sells bananas or what, he buys *pombe* or meat. You know how we Anyalungu people value meat. We tend to hate *maharagwe* or *tajuni.*"

Nobody joined in immediately after this. All the guests kept looking on and merely listening. They actually found the talk sickening but they let it go on, propelled by forces they couldn't control.

Then slowly Alkarim began, thoughtfully. "And you know, when I just returned from Pwani those days, I put up small shop. But the jealousy of people, only Allah knows. I wanted to die just like a rat. But I kept saying that our benefactor, Allah gives to those he chooses. And today they look at me as if it was not they who did it." He continued. "And have you ever got news of that son of Lubele?" he said, this time his mood wholly changed.

"Which one?" Mihanyo, the famous *jumbe* of pre-*Uhuru* times, took it over.

"I am not talking to you," Alkarim told the lengendary employee of the D.C. "I am asking you, Mulenge, about your son-in-law. Didn't I hear that Lunja has betrothed your daughter, Moina?"

Mulenge did not say anything. He looked up once and when he saw that Alkarim was no longer fixing eyes on him, turned his eyes away.

Alkarim continued, "My son, Zalembe, went to Daisalama and met Lunja there. He says that it was just by accident. Lunja was dressed in tatters, rotten tatters. Zaleme asked him 'Where do you live?' Lunja could not show him. These children cheat you all the time. And as for

the Anyalungu girls, to hear of Daisalama, they tremble as if it is to see a god. When do you marry your daughter to him?" Alkarim teased Mulenge.

But Mulenge found it no joke. His face darkened, half in grimace and half in indignation.

"And I tell you when Lunja comes to marry, the day of marriage you will think that he is the biggest boss in the whole of Daisalama. He will borrow all sorts of things. Radios, suits, everything. Ha! Why, don't I know the *wahunis* of Pwani?"

By the afternoon a big crowd had gathered at Hamniwezi. On the open ground in front of the shop, the Anyalungu girls' dance was in full swing. A lot of boys came from as far as Mbazala and Mkomolo. They crowded around the circle of the girls and admired them greatly. The girls danced very beautifully and their hips undulated with skill. Simon was there, too. He stood on the outermost ring and stole several looks at Moina, who appeared to dance most skillfully and attracted the attention of all boys.

At Hamniwezi, the celebrations and drumming went on and on that evening. The noise of rejoicing went echoing in the Mpunguta hills. The bright light that came from the petromax hanging in front of the Hamniwezi restaurant was courteous to the *bao* players under it, and also favoured those who sold foodstuffs to the celebrating crowd.

By midnight the moon was high in the sky and the dancing seemed to have just started. Amina, in her bedroom, had tried to sleep but the rejoicing outside appeared to disturb her endlessly. She tried hard to close her eyes but she couldn't. Then she got vaguely nervous. She dressed up hurriedly and went out. Zaleme was sitting on the verandah playing the *bao*. She called him.

"How, now?" she asked. "Does this mean that we are not going to have even some little sleep today? I'm tired with this yelling. Tell them to go away now. This is not Orofea." Saying this she turned and, going into her room, she threw herself on the soft mattresses. The noise outside faded slowly and in the next ten mintes the crowd had dispersed, leaving the compound very quiet.

Still Amina could not get any sleep. Her eyes were just too dry.

Kadufi, wrapped in his heavy calico sheets and blankets, strolled along the verandah looking for some dark place to hide himself and go to sleep. He walked to the corner facing the poultry house and gave himself a good camouflage behind some wooden boxes. He lay his spear and some other weaponry on top of the boxes.

There had been a noise outside the house of Muyeya soon after midnight. Then there was the clucking of the fowls. After five minutes or so the clucking ceased. Muyeya had listened to the noise, not without a throbbing heart. It was similar to that produced by a light animal moving on dry leaves. He thought that it might have been a goat that had been let loose. He ignored it.

Then minutes later the same noise came from the poultry house of Alkarim. The great number of fowls made such a big noise that the whole household awoke. It was a leopard. It had come all the way down from the Mpunguta hills, trying to break into animal sheds to steal goats. Now it had reached the compound of Alkarim and was finding a way to steal chickens. Kadufi had then been asleep about two hours. Kadufi, as watchman, had been the first to wake up. His hair stood on end as he raised himself above the short verandah wall and peeped. The black spots on the skin of the animal showed very distinctly in the moonlight. He went down again and curled up neatly, close to the wooden boxes. The clucking continued and with the cocks taking part, amplified, finally breaking into pandemonium.

Alkarim woke up. He came near to a window in a room that faced the poultry house and peeped.

"Kadufi!" he called many times. Kadufi, who was at the boxes just below the window, was afraid to make the least noise. He merely grunted faintly.

"What is it? Are you sleeping at a time of work? Kadufi! Do you sleep?" Alkarim became desperate.

The leopard ran all round the shed and Alkarim caught sight of it. He, too, did not fail to recognise it. Other members of the household had awakened. The son and daughters-in-law and others crowded in the backyard. When Alkarim heard their voices, he dashed from the window and hurried to apprise them of the danger.

"Don't go out!" he yelled at Zaleme and Juma, who were already opening the door. "Don't, it is a leopard! Keep all the doors closed." Then with the sons he came back to the window.

"Where is Kadufi?" Juma asked.

"The fool is sleeping here below the window."

"I can't see him," Zaleme wailed, peeping more closely. He took out a long stick and poked Kadufi with it. Kadufi grunted again.

"Wake up, foolish. Take your weapons. Now!"

Alkarim was furious. He took over the stick from Zaleme and with it knocked over the weaponry from the boxes where they lay.

"It is a leopard, danger!" Kadufi -whispered, opening his mouth for the first time.

"Now go and chase it. Are you afraid?"

"Ah, *Baba*, this is very dangerous, *Baba*," he whispered again, this time barely audible. The leopard succeeded in getting hold of one cock and disappeared. But the clucking of the terrified hens increased. Alkarim wanted to come outside and pull out Kadufi but he feared that the animal was still around.

"Where is this Kadufi?" the women asked Zaleme. "He is sleeping under the boxes."

"Why do you not tell him to go and chase it? He should kill it!" Amina insisted.

"He doesn't want to. I have ordered him many times but he is very stupid." Alkarim said in disappointment.

"We always tell you that Kadufi is not a good servant, dismiss him. But you don't hear us. When we are all busy here and ask him to do one kind of work or other he refuses," the wife of Zaleme reported.

"Oh," the wife of Juma took it up, "that's not a lie. Yesterday I asked him to go and fetch water, he gave the pretence that he was not well. I know that he was not willing."

Alkarim, who had been standing and holding the long stick in his hands as he listened, then returned to the window. He peeped and found Kadufi still clinging to the side of the box.

"Kadufi from now I am going to 'have another watchman. You should never be seen on my premises and I don't want to see you again."

Kadufi threw the heavy blankets off. It shocked him to hear that he had lost all value by a fault he did not admit. He was now no more afraid of the animal. Standing up and facing Alkarim, who was still peeping, he spoke, all the vehemence in him exhibiting his voice.

"Kamuyuga, you are very stupid, *shenzi*. You are a great thief. You are nobody other than a thief and you took part in the murder of that Indian. You are proud of stolen property and you cheat the people that this business has come out of selling bananas which you carried on your head. I don't care! I know what I can do and you will suffer. We shall see!" Finishing-this he got up and, taking the weaponry in his hands, slung the sheets over his shoulder, and marched away in the moonlight.

None 'among the women said anything. By the time Kadufi disappeared, they had already got in their rooms and listened through half-open doors.

"He will see," Alkarim said. "I say he will repent and the time he will do it will be too late!"

They went to bed. Alkarim did not fall asleep soon. It was not before three in the morning when slowly his eyes closed and they did not open again until next morning at ten when his wife Amina came to wake him up.

"People want you outside," she told him.

Outside there were three people. Saidi-wa-manamba, Mihanyo and Kadufi. He let them in and they sat on a mat in the backyard. It did not take much time before the other members of the household crowded to watch and listen. Some leaned against the walls and some pretended to busy themselves with their housework. Kadufi, who appeared to have brought the others with him, began to talk.

"I have called you elders here to come and help me apologise to my master. A wild animal came here yesterday and only through bewilderment I didn't kill it. Now I ask this Baba Alkarim to pardon me. You know we human beings are like that. It is ordinary for human beings to wrong others", he finished.

Saidi-wa-Manamba took over. "This Kadufi came to Mshenye before the first cock-crow to fetch me. He said that we should come by that hour but I said 'no'. Now, Bwana Alkarim, you know that this Kadufi is just like a child. He can't hold a hoe or what. You have been feeding him for many years already. He is now already old and you have taught him to live comfortably. Now . . ."

As Saidi-wa-Manamba continued his plea, Kadufi went rolling in the dust at the feet of Alkarim, which had protruded off of the mat. Kadufi kissed them as he rolled. "Now you say that you dismiss him. This means to ruin his life," Saidi finished. Kadufi, after rolling for three or four times, lay still.

Alkarim still kept quiet. He appeared to be thinking hard whether to accept him back or not. The whole compound then became all quiet. Kadufi did not take his eyes off the lips of Alkarim, which were to pronounce the sentence. They looked like the huge axe of the executioner ready to strike.

"I forgive him," Alkarim began slowly. "But if there has been any damage done by that animal, then he should repair it. Only that."

"Thanks a lot, Father," Kadufi murmured in Anyalungu as he repeated the rolling and kissing of the feet of Alkarim, this time more profusely than before.

Alkarim went to the poultry house to check the stock. Sooner or later, he noticed that the biggest cock called Muhuni was not there.

"Muhuni is not here," Alkarim said, turning to face the three old fellows, who, by then, stood behind him.

"Muhuni, that big cock?" Kadufi murmured, apparently shocked.

"Up to now only Muhuni is missing."

"Ah, that's no matter, *Baba*, thanks a lot."

TWENTY

A bus sped along the tarmac road from Dar es Salaam on one fine morning and gained speed as time elapsed. The spongy seats bumped up and down comfortably. It was a new bus and printed on the side in block capitals was DAR-BULEMBE, above the owner's name—B. J. KHANJI & SONS.

Lunja Lubele was squeezed near a window. The bus sped up past Magomeni, the workers' neighbourhood where the elder son of Lubele then lived in a rented room. Lunja was caught by the feeling that he should get off the bus and walk to his room, the window of which came to his eyes at that moment. He had that emptiness a person gets when leaving his home, his property and all those he loved, and going to a place from which he doesn't hope to return. Bulembe by then only existed in his dreams. It seemed for the most part a place he did not know. The many letters he had received telling him about many sad things made him get the feeling that hangs over a criminal when the time to face his executioner comes.

He wondered why he had not been able to go to Bulembe even once in all that time he had been away. Then memories flashed through his mind. He traced his whole life from that day he left Bulembe until the moment he was sitting in the bus. He recalled his life as a *manamba* in Tanga, as a house-boy in Arusha. where he taught himself how-to read and write. Then in the sugar plantations at Arusha *Chini*. After Arusha *Chini*, Lunja had joined a transport organisation, where he had not been paid for many months and at last decided to quit. There were some adventures in Moshi and he learnt a good deal about different things, and it was at that time when the hooliganism he had thrown himself into began to part slowly and gave way to settled, manly ideas.

From Moshi, Lunja went straight to Dar es Salaam where, usually, he found employment with various building contractors and acquired good experience in masonry. This was the work it seemed he most enjoyed.

The bus sped on and they passed Kibaha. Lunja crane his neck to the side and peeped through the bus window. His eyes caught the glimmer of some white buildings. He remembered a time he had lived there. He had worked in the construction of the buildings that then stood before his eyes. From the distance came the sight of some student playing on what looked, from the distance, like football field. Others strolled around, listlessly watching those who played. He had stayed at the place for a long time but by then the whole experience was only a flicker in his memory. And he realized that time was something mobile. The vision was abruptly cut off when the bus went round a corner.

A little after seven that day, the bus pulled up before the shop of Khanji. It was not dark yet. Simon had been there strolling about the short street, awaiting the arrival of his brother. Lunja alighted and the two brothers were soon on their way to Majengo.

"Did you know that I would arrive today?"

"Oh, why not? You mentioned today's date in that last letter you wrote me."

Lunja found everything very much new to him. He was anxious to explore the town at the earliest opportunity. They reached Majengo. Simon switched on the torch he had in his hand and the light fell on his door. They went in and laid down the luggage. Simon lit the lantern and now the brothers got a chance to examine each other more closely. Lunja had become a serious, cool person. He asked few questions and talked little. He had no longer those feature that belonged to what the Anyalungu called a "youth". He was past the age an Anyalungu male got married. He also had grown a moustache. Simon found his brother very much changed from when he left him that year, 1963, when Simon came to work as TANU secretary at Bulembe.

"How are Father and Mother?" he asked Simon.

"They are all well. But Father is not a very happy man as he used to be those days. He doesn't talk to people and it seems that all people avoid him." Lunja only listened. He didn't comment for the time, although his eyes revealed things going on in him.

"And have you been meeting any Mpunguta people in Dar es Salaam?" Simon continued.

"Ah, no. I only met Zaleme one day. I was at work and he appeared to be in a burry. We talked only briefly."

Lunja was very tired, having sat on the bus for a whole day. He took off his shoes and stretched himself on the bed. His eyes fixed at the ceiling. Simon continued to speak of their father.

"Father doesn't pass by the house of Kamuyuga. When he comes to town he takes a route through the bush. You know Kamuyuga has influenced all people to look down upon him. And also he speaks very badly of him. Now everybody fears Kamuyuga, such that nobody can afford to be seen co-operating with Father or even greeting him."

When Simon finished this, the room fell into an oppressive silence. Lunja brought out a cigarette and began to smoke.

"How about that girl you have been writing me about?"

"She is called Moina, the daughter of Mulenge. I hope that you still remember Mulenge. But now, you know, there seems something going on. Kamuyuga has been giving a lot of things to the girl and her parents, presents and many things. And I have heard that Kamuyuga himself wants to make her as a second wife. I wanted to ask her about this some few days ago when I met her and talked to her of your coming, but my tongue just didn't speak out the words."

"Do you think I can see her tomorrow?" Lunja asked.

"Why not? We will, send for her when we reach Nlimanja."

They went on talking thus for a long time. After taking their supper they stretched themselves on the beds that lay by the walls and continued talking. Simon narrated all that had taken place when Lunja was at Pwani, all that occurred in Mpunguta and Bulembe in general, about the work

he was doing then. He spent a long time telling him about Alkarim and his sons, about Saidi-wa-manamba and lastly about Moina.

Next day was a Saturday and Simon came home from work in the early afternoon. They took their meal and immediately started off for Mpunguta. They walked hurriedly and talked little. When they neared Mpunguta they halted at the signboard. Their eyes dwelt upon the word HAMNIWEZI. They stared at the board for a long time. Then Lunja asked his brother, as they began walking on again, "What is this Hamniwezi?"

"Didn't I tell you that this is the residence of Kamuyuga? He calls himself Hamniwezi, the invincible, and hence the name of all his property. His shop, butcheries, restaurants and even his sons are referred to by the same appellation."

"And what about this other name—Alkarim?"

"Ohoo-Kamuyuga is no more what you may have been knowing. I really wonder how you never had news of him, a personality so remarkable."

"But what made him call himself Hamniwezi?"

"Ohoo—maybe what I am telling you is not enough to make you understand. You will have to see it for yourself," Simon said, laughing.

At Hamniwezi there was the characteristic crowding of people. They lingered about on the verandahs of the place lazily. Some sat on the chairs of the restaurant, their throats parched with thirst. Hunger enslaved them. They kept looking at each other and would fix their eyes on anybody who bought himself something to eat. Then they would keep watching as he ate until all went down the gullet. Saidi- wa-Manamba was there playing the *bao* and Alkarim himself was standing on the doorsteps. There was an uneasy silence punctuated by the music that blared from a huge radio lying on a shelf in the restaurant.

Lunja halted and greeted the owner of all this wealth.

Alkarim didn't respond and instead the coarse voice of Saidi-wa-Manamba took up the greeting. Without wasting more time they started down the hill to the Mfele valley. Saidi raised his head and looked hard at Lunja who was walking behind Simon.

"I don't think that I know this boy. Who is he?" He asked this loudly enough that Lunja himself heard. And Alkarim answered him in the same loud voice, his eyes following Lunja with scorn.

"Ah! this is our *mheshimiwa*"

Lunja let the comments flow past him. He remained unperturbed with the deep impassivity he now possessed. The brothers went on.

An hour or so later, Simon went to the house of Mulenge. He did not go right into the compound. He had been able to call Moina through her younger sister, who was found sitting in front of the house.

Simon and Moina stood along the path from the river. He informed her about the arrival of Lunja and that she should see him that evening. Moina kept digging holes with her big toe in the sand where she stood. She did not seem much interested in what Simon had been telling her.

"Will you then be able to come this evening or what?"

"I don't know."

"How do you fail to know? If you don't know about yourself, who do you expect to?"

"I don't know if I will be free by then."

Simon became annoyed. He got the feeling that Moina no longer loved Lunja. He wondered why she did not speak it out and kept teasing him instead. The mother of Moina passed them, carrying a bucket. Simon greeted her as he got out of her way. Moina, for a time, kept her eyes fixed at her mother as the elder woman disappeared down the hill. The toe now stopped digging. Instead Moina began pulling out the grass growing by the side of the path.

"There is nothing to worry about saying what you feel Moina. You are not tied. Say, now, will you come?" Simon asked, this time in a much changed tone.

"I don't know," she said again, bending down and chewing the grass.

"All right. If you think you like or you don't, that's all up to you." Saying this, Simon departed.

A short time after Simon and Moina's meeting, Mulenge sat in his house at the fireside as his wife made the *ugali* for supper. After the meal the two parents resumed their positions at the fireside. Mulenge did not talk much and he appeared thoughtful. At length he called Moina. Moina came near to where her parents had sat. Mulenge said nothing for a long time. He cast his eyes at the fire as if he was afraid to say the thing he had called Moina for. At last he began coldly.

"Moina, what were you talking about with that rogue? Look here, you child. You can't break my relation with. Alkarim and put me to shame. I have always told you that you are not a child to fail to choose a good husband for yourself.

"I told you many times that I don't want to see you with the children of Lubele. The youth you say is your fiance, Lunja, we hear that he is just a houseboy of some Indian in Daisalama. I have heard that Zaleme, when he went there that time, he met Lunja in tatters. Now you want him to be your husband."

Moina did not say anything. She looked down and her neck bent as if suffering indignation. Her mother took over.

"Alkarim wants to marry you and you say you don't want him because he is old. What has old age to do with a husband? Does he turn into a tree? He loves you and you should love him, too. Alkarim will give you everything you want. Your word will turn the law in the whole house. You will only sit and servant like Zayumba will fall at your feet!"

"Not only Zayumba," Mulenge poured in. "Say all the house. The shops and everything will be yours. Now I tell you one last thing. Today Alkarim has sent his mission to me to remind me about the marriage. Alkarim has told me that he doesn't want to hear any nonsense about you with the sons of Lubele or he will break the engagement. I have answered his mission that I recognize Alkarim as my son in-law. If you will not follow what I tell you then you cease to be my daughter. I don't want to hear anything about your rogues."

They continued to talk on the same subject for a long time. They asked the girl what Simon had been talking to her about that afternoon and Moira told as much as she thought she could.

The morning, very early, Simon went to Bulembe to fetch the luggage his brother had left behind the day before. Lunja woke up quite early, too. The old man, Lubele, had not awakened and therefore Lunja strolled about the compound, looking at the various things that came to be there during his absence. He only fixed his eyes on them but his thoughts were buried under an avalanche of things that came into his head, one after another.

Then something caught his eye and completely broke the order of his thoughts. He saw Moina descending the hill with a bucket in her hands. He, without giving thought to it, started down the hill as well, and the two arrived at the river almost at the same time.

"Moina, how are you?"

"I am all well."

"You appear to be uneasy about something or other, or are you not?"

"There is nothing wrong. I am not feeling uneasy," she said, trying as hard as she could not to look at Lunja. Lunja walked on the bare earth rock and came near to Moina.

"I heard you said you would come to Nlimanja yesterday. What happened to you, after all?"

"I didn't say I would come. Who told you?"

Lunja did not add anything. Moina let the bucket fall into the river and bent herself, resting her face on her lap. Lunja came near to her on the bare rocks and stood behind her.

"Don't stand close to me like that," she warned him.

"Why so, Moina?"

"Please, please Lunja don't." Moina was serious about it. She stood up and faced Lunja, her eyes burning. "You know you can be seen standing near me and things may go very bad with you if Alkarim hears this." Moina swung around to see if there was anybody watching. Then she took four strides away from Lunja. She went on speaking with the same look on her face.

"You know a person may happen to come down the hill or peep at us from the bush and when he sees us here standing like that, it may be very dangerous. Particularly if Alkarim hears about it"

Lunja did not say anything more. He had wanted to burst out and say something or other but a sudden force took the better of him. His head was raised up and his eyes seemed to pierce the heavens.

Moina immersed the bucket and pulled it out as it filled. With the bucket balancing on her head she started up the hill and Lunja, who was by then standing a distance away, gave way to her absentmindedly. She went up and up the hill and disappeared, leaving Lunja fixed in the same spot.

TWENTY-ONE

Alkarim didn't feel it safe to let Moina continue to live out of his compound when Lunja was at Nlimanja. Four days after the arrival of Lunja he took the girl's hand in marriage. The scene at Hamniwezi was filled with people. They ate, drank, sang and danced in celebration. But the celebrations didn't last long. There was not much cheering, particularly among the young people. Even the Alkarim family itself didn't look happy about the marriage.

Lunja spent all his time at Nlimanja. There were occasions when he visited his young brother in the town. Since after the arrival of Lunja, Lubele had completely- changed his attitude towards Simon. When Simon came to Nlimanja to see his brother, Lubele did not talk to him. He would straightaway go to bed without even greeting him. Eventually Simon became aware of this and discussed it with his brother. When Lunja had completed a two-week stay, Lubele caught an illness. He spent all the time sleeping. Simon came to Nlimanja one afternoon after work. The old man was sleeping inside. Simon entered. But when Simon greeted him, Lubele didn't answer. Immediately after Simon had stepped into the room, Lubele rolled the blanket over his head, which had before stayed uncovered.

The following morning, Lunja went to help his mother with her weeding in the fields. His mother appeared very moody and they talked about various things. At noon Nganda went back home and made a meal which she brought to the field. Lunja stopped working for a moment and they sat under a shade tree taking their lunch.

While they ate, the mood of Nganda changed rapidly. She chewed a single lump for a long time. Her eyes were fixed at the uprooted weeds lying in heaps in front of her. She wandered far and near in her thoughts. Then gradually she came back to herself. "Your father is becoming more and more ill with many thoughts. He is more sad than ill," she said, still looking at the assembled weeds.

"What is he thinking of?" Lunja asked, throwing a glance at his mother.

"You ask why? You know it well enough, how do you dare to ask?" Nganda spoke very reproachfully. "Your father wrote you many years ago to come and get married. You didn't come, and now you are past the age of marriage. We are now very old and you, the sons, don't want to marry. Who do you think can take care of us?

"Your case is not so bad in the eyes of your father. But your young brother, Simon. When your father recalls the heavy baskets of bananas he carried on his head to Bulembe in order to pay his school fees at Mbazala, he sheds tears! Now Simon sank himself deep into TANU. What has he brought out of TANU? And it is TANU, too, that made your father break relations with his brother, Kamuyuga. Now all people laugh at your father. He feels so much ashamed even to talk with people. Was Lubele a person to feel shame before the people of Mpunguta? Do you still find this good?"

Nganda had stopped eating. She found no more taste in the meal. She went on.

"People have told your father that the friends of Simon who had been in TANU with him before *Uhuru* left TANU immediately after *Uhuru* and started building up shops and other businesses. And now they look masters front of people. But look at us, now. We are wearing away with hard work and what we get is still more poverty. Our whole life has been spent in torment. Do you think your father can stand in front of people and boast of an educated son?" Finishing this, Nganda broke into sobs.

The same morning, Zayumba had been sitting in the kitchen making *maandazi* for the restaurant. Some few businessmen arrived at Hamniwezi from Bulembe. Alkarim ordered the servant to make tea for the guests. Leaving aside the *maandazi*, Zayumba began to make tea.

When the tea was ready Zayumba fetched a tray and filled it with cups. He went back to the kitchen to fill the cups with the tea. At that moment, Moina—the newly married Mrs Alkarim—came out of her bedroom, which was part of the front house to the left of the shop, and walked towards the door that opened into the backyard. She walked leisurely, her head turned to the right, staring at the guests who by then were playing *bao* on the verandah outside. Zayumba, bent over the tea-filled cups on the tray, proceeded into the shop from the backyard. Moina approached the door from the side, without being seen by Zayumba on the other side of the wall, her head still turned towards the men. When Zayumba was already half-way through the door, Moina walked right into the tray. Her right arm, which she had been swinging. banged the underside of the tray and the cups slipped off. Zayumba struggled in vain to save them.

When Moina turned her head around, her eyes met the empty tray clutched by the hands of Zayumba. She looked down at the cement floor. All cups were turned into fragments. The tea that once filled them then flowed into tiny streams.

"Where do you put your eyes when you walk? Can't you even see people coming in front of you?" Moina shouted at him so loudly that the people playing *bao* outside could hear. When her voice came into the ears of Alkarim, he sprang from the mat and ran past the counter in a second.

"What has happened?"

Moina did not answer. She slung her *khanga* over her shoulder and walked into the backyard haughtily.

"See for yourself the way your servants handle your property," she said, without looking back.

"I will not say anything. Many times he has been careless. This time he will pay for the cups." Saying this Alkarim walked back to the *bao*.

All this time Zayumba., had remained quiet. He walked back into the kitchen, his face turned down.

"Can't you see that the shop floor needs decking? We don't want flies buzzing in the shop," Moina kept pressing upon him.

Fetching a bucket, Zayumba walked down the hill towards Mfele.

Zayumba spent a long time at the river. He bent over the bucket, staring at his reflection in the water. Whenever he wanted to lift the bucket and walk back to Hamniwezi, he felt short of strength. Then, without knowing what he was doing, he squatted beside the bucket and concentrated upon the reflection in the water. However, he did not dwell on the image. His thoughts seemed to pierce his forehead: he was reciting what was stored under his skull.

His face quivered under the tension of the things that passed in his head. The many years he had served women of different races opened up before him, bit by bit. He was extremely depressed. His blood began to flow faster and faster as fresh feelings came back to him. Moina, that mere child, could she really do that to him? Sweat began to form on his forehead. Then he came to his conclusions. He stood up and ascended the hill.

Moina was sitting in the backyard before a huge mirror, plaiting her hair. Then, in the mirror she saw the image of Zayumba as he stepped into the backyard. There was no bucket on his head. She sprang from the chair she had been sitting on and let fall the comb she had in her hand.

"*Alaa! Ushenzi gani huu?*" she cursed, walking closer to Zayumba.

Zayumba turned to face her. His eyes reddened. Before Moina could add another word more, the huge left palm of the veteran houseboy and *maandazi*—maker had gripped her hair, which had been combed up in a single huge tuft, and by his right hand he sent a full-strength blow onto her back. Moina dropped flat onto the ground. He raised her and gave her a second blow. She went down again on her chin. And, raising her a third time he pushed her backwards. She knocked against the chair and mirror and fell, lying stretched out next to the chair. He lifted her again and another blow sent her to the wall. She hit the wall and fell. Zayumba was coming upon her again when one of the Bulembe businessmen grabbed him. But Zayumba proved stronger. He freed himself and kicked the new bride of Alkarim with his right leg. Moina went rolling in the dust.

More people came to the rescue of Moina. But they could not come near Zayumba. He threatened to kill anybody who would touch him. Alkarim, shaking all over, managed to pick up Moina in his arms and half drag her into the shop. Once inside the shop, Alkarim dropped the bolt.

The rest of the Alkarim family, who had been lounging in the backyard, had by then disappeared. They had all locked themselves up in the bedroom of Zaleme in the back-house. In the backyard were left only the Bulembe shopkeepers, some two passersby who had been attracted by the incident, and Zayumba. Zayumba went to the door and banged it with his fists.

"Give me my salary!" he roared. "All the money for my five years' work. Or else I will kill you today." The voice of Zayumba had altogether much changed. His eyes flashed fire.

Alkarim, feeling assured of his safety behind the huge shop doors, replied. "I swear that you will not get any money and I don't want you here anymore!"

"You will give it."

"I will not.

"All right." Finishing this Zayumba marched out of the backyard and disappeared.

"Bwana Alkarim," said one of the two men. "He has gone away now. You can just come out."

"No. I will not come out. If you want, come in and let's shut ourselves inside here. It is safer inside here." He pulled up the bolt and opened the door for his visitors.

"Nobody should stay out. Anybody may be killed today," he shouted at those locked in the bedroom of Zaleme.

"But why all this trouble, Bwana Alkarim?" one of the shopkeepers asked when they were seated inside the shop. "Why did you not dismiss him the first time you found him useless?"

"He is really useless," another visitor took it up. "And the tea you ordered him to bring to us, did he make any? Too much saliva has been pouring down our gullets. Is this respect, you think?"

Alkarim did not answer. His limbs were still trembling.

The town people continued.

"These days servants are not a thing to look for. I tell you, Samuel, at Ngaza, everyday people run away from his farms because of the way he treats them. Yet everyday his compound is filled with job-seekers. Then why do you trouble with this leopard?"

"And indeed he is a devil. His eyes!" Alkarim spoke, still shaking. "I never knew that I had been keeping such a beast in my own house."

What had taken place at Hamniwezi that morning became known all over Mpunguta by that same noon. The news had spread like wind. In every house people talked about Zayumba and Moina.

That afternoon Simon walked slowly towards the village. He had guessed the feelings of his father even before Lubele stopped speaking to him. His neck was bent forward and his eyes were cast onto the little path as he walked on. He thought of TANU. He had been serving quite a long time then. At the time at he joined it, TANU was engaged in the Independence movement. *Uhuru* for the people. Then his thoughts dwelt upon the personalities of Bangama and Sengene. Then he thought of Samuel. What type of people were they, really?

When he neared Mpunguta he heard much noise coming from Hamniwezi. His reflections broke up and he marched faster. As he came nearer and nearer the noise increased. There was a lot of jeering and hooting. People had filled the Hamniwezi restaurant and those who didn't get space inside stood outside with the women. Simon found out that even people of Mkomolo who had by chance been passing had stopped there, too.

Simon slipped through the crowd and peeped through the doorway. Something struck him even more than the crowd itself. He saw among the assembly his father, leaning against one of the walls. "The sick man has come too!" Simon gasped.

Alkarim was sweating. Around him were the Bulembe shopkeepers who came that morning, and members of his morning and members of his family. Everyone seemed tense.

"I say that he will not get his salary," Alkarim kept repeating to the hooting and jeering crowd, banging the tables with his fists. "Let him go to the TANU secretary as you advise him. Isn't the TANU secretary his brother-in law? Let him go. If it is to complain to TANU, then I am also a TANU member." Saying this Alkarim fetched a membership card and held it out to show the people. He went on shouting.

"Go there. Go. If you think that you can use the influence of your *shemejis*, then I tell you that all the officers you see in Bulembe are under my influence. Ask anyone."

At this crowd jeered again. " *Mpee . . .* , *mpee ...*" they yelled.

Andunje also began to demand his pay for tilling the whole valley at Mfele. The whole multitude then cried, "*atoe...atoe...*" The Zayumba affair had sparked off something that had lain dormant in the hearts of the people. And that day they had turned into completely different people.

Even before Andunje finished forwarding his claims, Kadufi had had joined him.

"Kamuyuga," he said, emphasising, the African name, "I want my money. My salary cannot have been food and tea only!" Kadufi had become very serious. He stepped forward in the face of the son of Kahocho. When he called Alkarim by the old name, Kamuyuga, everybody became mad with excitement. They all shouted.

"*Toa*, Kamuyuga . . . *toa!*" From then every voice referred to him as Kamuyuga.

Alkarim became mad with anger. His body shook with exasperation. His jaws became stiff and for a moment he couldn't speak. He pushed Kadufi with such force that Kadufi fell on his buttocks. At that, the people laughed merrily. Nobody helped him to his feet. However, their attitude towards Alkarim didn't change in the least. They went on shouting. "*A toe . . . atoe . .* "

"Now go out," Alkarim shouted. "Get out, all of you. My hotel is beginning to smell of shit. Away all of you, *shenzi,*" he said, pushing the crowd in front of him.

But the crowd pushed back, too.

"*A toe . . . atoe . . .*" they went on shouting.

Simon, who until then had remained unnoticed by the excited crowd, quietly slipped off from the scene. Outside the restaurant he caught hold of *Mzee* Muyeya and asked what had happened. Muyeya related the whole case. Inside the restaurant, Alkarim still struggled with the crowd. Agony was clear on his face.

After hearing the case from *Mzee* Muyeya, Simon walked out of the compound and down the hill towards his father's home. There was nobody at Nlimanja. All had gone to Hamniwezi. Then he pulled up a chair and sat outside the house, gazing at Hamniwezi across the valley. The noise from Mpunguta grew bigger and bigger. It entered his ears faintly as his thoughts wandered far off. He flashed back to the colonial times and pictured life in those days. Then he came to those times when people all over the country talked about *Uhuru*. That was the time when he joined TANU. Even those who lacked the least idea of what *Uhuru* could mean found the word relief-bearing. It also carried much hope. The people took it to be a time when they would rid themselves of the claws of oppression.The D.C. and his accomplices would fall, and with them all the scandal. The subjugated would then take over, a happy new society!

But it was clear that there was no freedom yet. For the ordinary man, peasant or worker, freedom was still beyond reach. And the word *Uhuru* had suddenly become vague. His office had day after day been full of complaints. It appeared that the colonial masters had hatched numerous emulators and, unfortunately, these emulators were right in the midst of their victims They knew the lives of their victims right from the cradle, where they would be strong and where they would be weak. Thus these were found to be even worse than the D.C. and his company. It was no longer a time when one would escape from the *boma* and the stooges of the D.C., and find relief and an air of freedom in the bush, even for the briefest while, and enjoy some joke with a companion.

This was the time when the dreaded D.C. was one's own neighbour, a relative. There was always someone near you to want to use you for something or other.

Simon turned his head to the right and looked at the compound at Hamniwezi. The noises now grew wilder. Then he swung round and sent a searching look all over the village up to as far as the Mpunguta hills. The houses showed no life. The whole population had assembled at Hamniwezi.

Simon discerned something quite distinct in the people. It was the feeling produced by the monster who towered over them with so much weight. The brothers, with coins for their everything. But unfortunately, to many, in their ignorance, it only appeared over them as a deep, black cloud. It could not be interpreted as a social structure constructed upon a clearly delineated ideological foundation. They did not conceive of a counter ideology to help dismantle the structures of oppression. But now Simon thought that he understood better. TANU had not fulfilled its task. The Party had seized the country from the whites, but it had not delivered it to the rightful owner. There was still a long way to go. The *Uhuru* they had achieved had only been a foundation stone. He could detect, too, a huge storm that had been silent in the course of gathering force. A storm that might not take long to break. This was only the eve of the storm, as was clearly seen on the peoples' humiliated faces. A craving by every soul ... they craved for the true *Uhuru*, the real Revolution.